HOW I SURVIVED MIDDLE SCHOOL

Can You Get an F in Lunch?

HOW I SURVIVED MIDDLE SCHOOL

Can You Get an F in Lunch?

By Nancy Krulik

SCHOLASTIC INC.
New York Toronto London Auckland Sydney
Mexico City New Delhi Hong Kong Buenos Aires

ISBN-13: 978-0-439-02555-3
ISBN-10: 0-439-02555-9

Published by Scholastic Inc.
SCHOLASTIC and associated logos are trademarks and/or registered trademarks of Scholastic Inc.

12 11 10 9 8 7 6 5 4 3 2 1 7 8 9 10 11 12/0

Printed in the U.S.A. 40
This edition first printing, June 2007
Book design by Jennifer Rinaldi and Alison Klapthor

For Mandy and Ian,
always my inspiration

Are You Ready for Middle School?

It's the night before your first day in sixth grade. Do you:

A. Call all your pals and arrange to walk to school together — there's safety in numbers?
B. Spend the whole night opening and closing your combination lock so you won't have trouble at your locker first thing in the morning?
C. Scarf down a pint of rocky road ice cream — nothing soothes stress like marshmallows, chocolate, nuts, and nougat?

You wake up in the morning and discover a massive zit in the middle of your forehead. Do you:

A. Get your best friend to swipe her big sister's makeup and then help you cover up the big bad blemish?
B. Put a Band-Aid over it and tell everyone you had a head-on collision with a door?
C. Hide under your bed?

Your math teacher has asked everyone to find a study partner to work with for the first marking period. Math is not your best subject. Do you:

A. Choose your best friend as your partner? You might not get the best grades, but at least you'll have fun working together.

B. Team up with the class math whiz? Then, once he's got your grades up, you can show him the ins and outs of coolness.

C. Find the most popular girl in your class and suggest the two of you become partners? Being seen together will definitely raise your social status.

So, How Ready Are You?

If most of your answers were A's, you're a lucky girl. You're headed for middle school with a BFF. So no matter how weird things get, you two will always be able to help each other pick up the pieces.

If most of your answers were B's, you're a creative gal who's got a solution for every problem. You'll be off to a great new year.

If most of your answers were C's, take a chill pill. You're going to middle school, not war. It's gonna be just fine, as long as you learn to relax, feel good about who you are, and trust your own judgment.

Chapter ONE

THE FIRST THING I NOTICED when I walked into Joyce Kilmer Middle School was Addie Wilson's red-and-white T-shirt.

Well, not the T-shirt actually. It was more the way Addie looked in the T-shirt. It was kind of short and moved up just past Addie's belly button when she raised her arm to wave to somebody down the hall. She looked like a pop star on MTV.

I looked down at my oversize green-and-white Camp Kendale T-shirt, the one with the lizard and the mountain on the front, and freaked out. I looked bad. Really bad. Like a big green tent with a head popping out of the top.

It's not like I'd planned on looking so bad when I'd picked out my clothes for the first day of school. When I left for school in the morning, I thought that wearing a T-shirt from a sleepaway camp was kinda cool. Not too many other sixth graders had been brave enough to go away to camp for a whole summer.

But me, I hadn't been afraid. Not at all. (Okay, at least not after the first few nights, when the homesickness had worn off.)

So you see, that was why I'd put on the T-shirt. I thought it made me seem very cool. Wrong!

MIDDLE SCHOOL RULE #1:

A BIG GREEN T-SHIRT WITH A LIZARD ON THE FRONT IS NOT MATURE.

Not at all. Especially not compared to Addie's teenage – or at least *almost* teenage – shirt.

Well, maybe everyone would be too excited about the first day of school to notice how lame my shirt was.

At that moment, I really wished I'd called Addie last night to see what she'd planned on wearing. Then maybe we could have coordinated, and Addie could have saved me from looking like such a dork.

It wouldn't have been the first time Addie had come to my rescue. There was the time I'd fallen off my bike and cracked my front tooth. (Good thing it had only been a baby tooth!) She'd been the one to come to the dentist with me and hold my hand when the dentist pulled out what was left of my baby tooth.

And then there was the time she'd seen that skunk hiding in the bushes and pulled me away before I could be sprayed with stinky skunk juice.

Of course, I'd done a lot of nice things for Addie, too. After all, she only lived two blocks away and we'd been best friends practically all our lives. We were almost the same age – I was three months older – and we'd always been in the same class at George Washington Elementary School.

In fact, the first time Addie and I had ever been apart for more than a week was this summer. I went to sleep-away camp, while she stayed home and went to day camp at the community center. I hadn't seen her since the morning I left for camp. When I got home in August, she and her family were already away on their annual beach vacation. Addie hadn't gotten back until yesterday morning, and I was excited to finally see her.

"Hey, Addie!" I shouted out as I ran down the hall toward her.

Addie turned and gave me a funny little grin. "Oh, hi, Jenny," she replied casually. Then, glancing at my T-shirt, she added, "I guess you had a good time at camp."

So much for no one noticing my shirt. But it was okay if Addie did. She knew me better than anyone.

"It was awesome," I told her excitedly. "Lots of hiking and outdoor camping. I even went on a canoe trip on the Delaware River. We went over real rapids! And when we went hiking, we got to go down a mud slide. It was the most incredible experience I ever had."

Addie made a face. "Mud slide? Like actually sliding down a hill of mud?"

"Yeah." I giggled, remembering what my bunk mates and I had all looked like after sloshing down the muddy slope. "It was awesome. We looked like mud monsters! I have some amazing pictures! I can't wait to show you."

When I finished talking, an uncomfortable silence fell over us like an itchy wool blanket. It was so strange. Usually Addie and I talked and talked and talked. We barely took time to breathe. Ordinarily, Addie would have had a million questions for me about what it had been like to be away from home for so long, and what kinds of activities I'd signed up for while I was at Camp Kendale.

At the very least, Addie would have told me all about her summer – especially since she'd been so busy she hadn't even had time to answer any of my letters. I frowned slightly, remembering how bummed out I'd been at mail call. On most days there would be a letter from my parents (usually with a dollar for the soda machine tucked inside the note) and a letter from a cousin, my grandmother, or maybe my friends Rachel and Felicia from school. But Addie never got a chance to write me. She must have had a really busy summer.

Still, that was okay. I figured Addie and I would talk when I got home. But things had been so crazy getting ready for school that we hadn't gotten the chance to talk at all – until now. And even now, Addie didn't have much to say to me. She was just biting her lip and playing with her hair.

Then, suddenly, it became totally clear. Addie was just as nervous about starting middle school as I was. Whoa. Addie Wilson, scared. *Incredible.*

It was almost impossible for me to picture Addie being nervous about anything. Usually Addie's the bravest person

I know. She always has been. In third grade, Addie became the first kid to ride a two-wheeler with no hands. Sure, she'd fallen off the bike and sprained her wrist, but still, she'd been the first. And then last year she'd been the only kid brave enough to go trick-or-treating at old Mrs. Morrison's creepy house. Addie was fearless.

But now, Addie was actually scared. I was absolutely, positively sure of it. The first day in sixth grade had her all freaked out. Why else would she be playing with her hair and looking nervously around the hallway.

"This is really exciting, isn't it?" I said finally, breaking the silence. I was trying to help Addie relax. "I mean, we're actually in middle school. *Sixth* grade. Wow. Just look at this place. There are lockers and everything. It's just like one of those schools on TV, you know?"

"Yeah," Addie agreed flatly. "The lockers are pretty cool."

"Where's yours?" I asked. "Hopefully we're right near each other. I've got locker 307."

"I'm 260," Addie said. "And I really should get there and put my things away. So . . ." she turned and started down the hallway.

"Oh, yeah, totally," I agreed. I looked at Addie. She still seemed kind of nervous. Sort of the way my pet mice look when they get spooked by a loud noise. "If you need any help opening your lock, just ask me. My dad and I were practicing all night. You just spin the dial a few times to the right, then stop on the first number. Then you turn the dial to the left and –"

"Jenny, I know how to open a lock," Addie said, as if she was annoyed with me. "Everybody knows how to open a lock." She sighed heavily. "Look, I have to –"

"Hey, Addie."

Just then, a tall boy with light brown hair and green eyes walked up beside us. He was wearing a community center swim team T-shirt. I guess Addie must have met him over the summer.

I waited for her to introduce us, but she didn't.

"What period do you have lunch?" the boy asked Addie.

"Fifth," Addie replied, her face suddenly lighting up. "How about you?"

"Me, too. Fifth period," he said. "Save me a seat?"

"Sure, Jeffrey," Addie promised.

"I have fifth period lunch, too," I said, trying to get into the conversation. "It must be a really popular lunch period."

Jeffrey stared at me for a minute. "Do I know you?" he asked.

"I don't think so," I answered. "I went to Washington Elementary School. You?"

Jeffrey turned his head. "I went to Lincoln. I'm in seventh grade."

"We probably never met then," I told him. "'Cause I went to Washington. But I'm in sixth grade now. Here, at Kilmer Middle School."

Jeffrey laughed. "Yeah, I kind of guessed you went here. After all, you're standing in the hallway."

Oh, man! I could feel the blood rushing into my cheeks. *Here, at Kilmer Middle School.* How could I have said something that stupid?

"This is Jenny McAfee," Addie told Jeffrey, finally introducing us. "She and I were in the same class last year."

"And the year before that, and the year before that," I added cheerfully. "Addie and I have always been in the same class."

"Oh, " Jeffrey said, immediately looking back at Addie. "I think Claire has fifth period lunch, too."

Addie nodded. "And Dana and Aaron. It's like the whole swim team got the same lunch period."

"Cool," Jeffrey said.

I'd only been away at Camp Kendale eight short weeks, but it looked like Addie had made a whole bunch of new friends. I obviously had a lot of catching up to do. But no problem. I'd just start meeting her new friends at lunch that afternoon. Before long, things would be back to normal.

"You know, I have English first period with Ms. Jaffe," Addie said, smiling at Jeffrey. "But I can't find the classroom anywhere."

"That's because Ms. Jaffe is in B wing, and this is C wing," Jeffrey told her. "I have to pass by her room on the way to my Spanish class. I'll take you there."

"I have Ms. Jaffe first period, too," I told Addie. "I know where her room is. My mom and dad took me on a tour of the building two days ago. I can show you –"

"That's okay," Addie said, turning down my offer with a strange little smile. "See you in class, Jenny," she added, as she turned and walked down the hallway with Jeffrey.

"Wait, I'll go with you," I called after her. But Addie must not have heard me, because she and Jeffrey never even turned around.

Chapter TWO

MIDDLE SCHOOL MORNINGS ARE LONG. Really long. In elementary school I ate lunch at 11:00 A.M. every day. And if the class got hungry before then, the teacher usually gave the class a snack at around 10:00 A.M. But not in middle school. No snacks here. And I had to wait until fifth period – 12:30 P.M. – to eat lunch.

It's not that 12:30 P.M. is that late or anything. But after spending the morning going up and down the stairs and from C wing to B wing and over to A wing, I'd worked up a big appetite. I was starved. So when the bell rang for fifth period I ran to my locker, got out my lunch, and . . .

Uh-oh. Slight problem.

I had no idea how to get to the cafeteria. The map in the school handbook was really confusing, and I had already taken so many wrong turns that most everyone had cleared out of the hallway. The only way I was gonna get to the cafeteria was ask someone for directions.

I'm not usually good at asking strangers for help. I'm kind of shy that way. But right then I was way hungrier than I was shy. When I spotted a group of older kids hanging out in the hall, I knew exactly what I had to do.

I took a deep breath and tried to think brave thoughts.

That was what my counselor at camp had told me to do whenever I had to try something new. At the time I had been scared to climb the high ropes or swim out to the far dock. But now I was going to have to think supercolossal brave thoughts if I was going to have to ask those kids where the cafeteria was. As I walked toward them I saw that both girls were wearing makeup, and the tall boy had dark fuzz peeking out from beneath his nose. I figured they were eighth graders. And everyone knew that eighth graders had no use for sixth graders.

Still, the way I looked at it, these eighth graders were my only hope of finding the cafeteria. It was either talk to them or starve!

"Um, excuse me," I said quietly as I walked up to them. My voice cracked just slightly, and I could feel my cheeks getting red-hot at the sound of it.

"Oh, Sonia, look, it's a sixth grader," laughed the red-haired girl.

"Nice shirt," her friend said sarcastically. She was thin, with brown hair and black eyeliner circling her eyes. "I like the chameleon."

"Actually, it's a lizard," I corrected her. "That's my camp's mascot. Camp Kendale. It's a *sleepaway* camp," I added, hoping to sound more cool.

It didn't work.

"Oh, a lizard," the brunette remarked. "Pardon me. I didn't mean to be insulting."

"Do you think lizards are insulted by being called chameleons, Kristin?" the redhead asked.

"I don't know, Sonia. I think maybe it's the other way around," Kristin replied with a giggle.

My cheeks were burning and I think a few beads of nervous sweat were forming on my forehead. I really hate it when people make fun of me. Not that anybody likes it, but I have a real problem with being made fun of. My mom says I have a "red button" when it comes to that. I don't know about a button, but I do know that my cheeks blush red faster than anyone in the universe! "It doesn't really matter . . ." I started to say, but my voice was suddenly drowned out by a large gurgling noise coming from my empty stomach.

"Ooh, I think the lizard's angry," Sonia joked. "It growled."

"Reptiles can be so sensitive." Kristin laughed.

I bit my lip really hard and blinked my eyes so I wouldn't cry.

"Did you want something, Lizard Girl?" the boy asked me.

"I'm . . . uh . . . I'm trying to find the cafeteria," I said in a voice so quiet it was almost a whisper. "I've been following this map they gave us in homeroom, but it just takes me around in circles and –"

"Oh, that's an old map," Kristin told me. "I think my mother had that one."

"Yeah, you'll never find the cafeteria from that thing," Sonia agreed. "That thing's so old, they don't even have the pool on that map."

"We have a pool?" I asked, amazed. No one said anything at orientation about a pool. I would have definitely remembered that.

"Sure," Kristin said. "You just take the elevator to the second floor, and it lets you off right near the pool. The cafeteria's right around the corner from there."

"Wow!" I exclaimed. "I didn't know we had an elevator, either."

"Lucky you bumped into us, huh?" the boy said. "Here's how you get to the elevator. Go all the way down this hall. Make a right. Then follow that hallway to the windows. Make a left and then a quick right. The elevator's right there. It'll take you to the pool and the cafeteria."

"Yeah, you can't miss it," Kristin added. "The elevator's the big gray metal door."

"Thanks!" I told them gratefully.

"No prob," Sonia answered.

As I walked down the hall toward the elevator, I held my head high. I had done it! I'd talked to eighth graders and lived to tell about it. Not only that, but because I'd been so brave I'd been rewarded with some facts that no other sixth grader seemed to know. We had a pool and an elevator in our school! I couldn't wait to tell Addie.

As I reached the end of the hallway I made a right turn. Then I headed for the windows, turned left, and then right.

Sure enough, there was the big gray door. Quickly, I looked around for the call button.

But there weren't any buttons or arrows or anything else on the door. Just the knob. *Maybe you have to open the door first*, I thought to myself as I reached to turn the doorknob. But the door wouldn't open. I jiggled the knob harder.

No luck. It was locked.

"Can I help you?"

I jumped as a tall man in a green uniform snuck up behind me.

"You okay?" The man asked me.

I gulped. "Yeah. Fine, I guess. I mean . . . um . . . you just scared me."

"Sorry. I was wondering what you were doing at my supply closet."

"Your what?"

"My supply closet. I'm the school janitor and that's my closet," he told me. "I don't know what you could possibly want in there."

"Nothing," I answered him quickly. "I mean, nothing but the elevator. I must have made a wrong turn or something. But these kids told me the elevator was at the end of this hall and it had a big gray door, so I figured . . ."

The janitor began to laugh. "The elevator," he repeated. "Those eighth graders do it every year."

Oh, man. I'd been punked. "So I guess there's no pool, either, huh?"

The janitor shook his head. "Nope. We do get some pretty deep puddles out on the soccer field, though."

I couldn't believe I'd fallen for that. Those eighth graders were probably laughing their heads off at me right now. They'd probably told half the school about the stupid sixth grader who'd fallen for the old elevator and pool trick.

"Don't feel too bad," he told me. "They only played that joke on you because someone did it to them when they were in sixth grade. And when you're in eighth grade, you'll probably do the same thing to some unsuspecting sixth grader."

But I wouldn't. Never.

"So what were you looking for?" the janitor asked, smiling.

"The cafeteria."

"You're about as far from that as you can get," he said.

Once again I could feel tears welling up in my eyes. I was such an idiot for believing them. And I was starving. Now it would take me forever to get to the other end of the school . . . if I could even find my way there. After all, I'd thrown out my map after those eighth graders told me it was outdated.

"Of course, you could cut through the teacher's parking lot and get there real fast," the janitor continued.

"But I can't leave the school building unless it's to go to the yard for recess," I insisted. "I saw it in the school handbook."

"You actually read that thing?" the janitor asked, surprised.

Of course I had read it. The whole thing. From cover to cover. I'd wanted to know everything about the school before I got there.

Unfortunately, the most important things you needed to know weren't in the handbook. Like what to wear on the first day or how to avoid being punked by eighth graders.

The janitor smiled kindly at me. "You can go anywhere in the school if you're accompanied by a staff member. So if you go through the parking lot with me, you'll be okay."

"You'd take me to the cafeteria?"

"Sure. Why not? I could go for a tuna hoagie right around now, anyhow," he replied. Then he held out his hand. "I'm Mr. Collins."

"Jenny McAfee." I shook his hand.

"Well, nice to meet you, Jenny," Mr. Collins said. "I think we're going to get along just fine. Most people say I'm a good person to know around here."

I smiled for the first time since I'd arrived at school. That was one thing I'd already figured out for myself.

Here's something else I figured out really quickly: A middle school cafeteria is nothing like an elementary school one. In elementary school, the kids sit with their class at long tables. And the teachers eat with their classes, too. Everyone is calm and quiet, using their "indoor voices."

But this cafeteria wasn't quiet or organized at all.

People were sitting all over the place – at tables, on the radiators, wherever they wanted. And they were loud. No indoor voices here.

Oh, yeah, I thought excitedly to myself. This was what middle school was all about!

"You gonna be all right?" Mr. Collins asked me.

I nodded. "I'm just looking for my friend's table. Thanks for getting me here."

"No problem," Mr. Collins replied. "I'm just gonna go get some lunch. Come find me if you need anything, okay?"

I nodded and smiled up at him. I was glad to finally know someone.

When Mr. Collins went to get his sandwich I was all alone again. I recognized a few of the kids at the tables, but I didn't see any of the kids Addie and I used to hang out with in our old school, like Rachel Schumacher or Felicia Liguori. They must have had lunch at a different period.

Most of the kids looked older than me. That was kind of scary. Back in elementary school, the fifth graders were the big kids. But now we were back to a place we hadn't been since kindergarten – we were the babies of the school.

When I spotted Addie in the crowd I felt relieved. She was sitting at a round table near the windows with Dana Harrison, a girl from our old school, Jeffrey the kid I'd met this morning, and a boy and a girl I didn't know, but they looked like seventh graders. I figured they had to be Claire and Aaron, the kids Addie had mentioned earlier.

I hurried over to the table, but as I got closer I noticed something kind of strange. There were no empty chairs. Had Addie forgotten to save me a seat? Nah. That couldn't be it. Back in elementary school Addie and I always sat together at lunch, usually with Felicia and Rachel. One of the older kids must've grabbed the last chair, and Addie was too nervous to explain that the seat was saved. I totally understood that.

"Hi, Addie," I said as I walked up to the table. "Sorry it took me so long to get here. I kind of got lost."

Suddenly everyone at the table stopped talking. They just stared at me.

"Oh, hi, Jenny," Addie said quietly.

"I'll just get a chair, and sit with you guys," I continued cheerfully. "I don't have to wait in line or anything. I brought my lunch."

"A brown bag lunch," Dana muttered. "Give me a break."

"What's wrong with a brown bag lunch?" I asked.

Dana shrugged. "Nothing, I guess. It's just that most people *buy* their lunch in middle school, you know?"

MIDDLE SCHOOL RULE #2:

No Brown Bag Lunches.

In fact, as I looked around the cafeteria, I did notice that most of the kids had cafeteria lunch trays in front of them. It was like a secret memo had been sent out to all the new sixth graders except me.

Okay. Starting tomorrow I'd bring money instead of lunch. But today I just wanted to eat. I was starving. I turned to the table next to Addie's and reached for an empty chair. "Are you using this?" I asked one of the boys who was sitting there.

"Nah. It's all yours," he replied.

"Cool," I said, taking the chair and swinging it over to where Addie was sitting. I stood there for a moment, waiting for Addie to move her chair and make room for me. But Addie didn't move over. No one at the table did.

"Um, we're kind of squished already," Addie told me quietly. "You got here kind of late."

Huh? I stood there for a moment. Had I heard Addie correctly? There was no room for me – *me* – at the table?

But judging by the way the other kids at the table ignored me, I'd heard her loud and clear.

Oh, man, the tears were coming again. How many times had I almost cried today? "Oh," I said quietly, blinking quickly to make sure none of the tears that were forming in my eyes would leak out onto my cheeks. "Sure. No problem. I'll . . . um . . . see you guys later."

I walked away from that table as fast as I could, with my brown bag lunch clutched in my hand. I looked around the cafeteria again, hoping to see someone I knew. Okay, so there was Mark Morgan and Justin Abramowitz, but I'd never really been friends with them. I spotted Olivia Becks sitting with some of her friends near the cafeteria door. Olivia had always been nice to me, even though she was a year older. But I hadn't seen her in a while and I didn't want to take a chance at getting rejected again.

Not that Addie had completely rejected me. I mean, it was sort of my own fault. I was the one who had come late, and the truth was, if I'd added another seat to that table, everyone would have been really squished.

But no matter what the reason, I was still without a lunch table. That meant I was going to have to eat lunch alone. But I couldn't. I just couldn't. What could possibly be more embarrassing than sitting all alone in the middle of this cafeteria while everyone else was eating with their friends? Everyone would be staring at me, wondering who the weird girl in the lizard shirt with no friends was.

I might as well stick a sign on my back that said LOSER. No way I was going to let that happen!

Then my stomach rumbled again – as if I needed a reminder that I was hungry. I had to eat lunch. I wasn't going to make it through the rest of the day without it.

And then I spotted it. A safe place. A place where no one would know what I was doing or saying. The phone booth! It was located in the corner of the cafeteria, right near the back exit of the school. I remembered from my school handbook that kids weren't allowed to use their cell phones in the school building, but we could make calls during lunch using the pay phone.

That was the answer! I zoomed over to the booth,

stepped inside, and shut the door. Then I took the phone off the hook and pretended to dial a phone number. As I gripped the phone between my shoulder and my ear, I sat down on the seat, opened up my brown bag, and took out my sandwich.

This was definitely not how I'd pictured my first lunch in middle school. I thought I would be sitting with friends, swapping stories, and laughing. But instead of hearing about summer vacations and school shopping sprees, the only conversation I heard was the sound of a recorded voice giving me the same message over and over: "If you'd like to make a call, please hang up and try again."

Chapter THREE

BY THE END OF THE SCHOOL DAY, my fingers were killing me from taking notes in class, my back hurt from carrying my book bag up and down the stairs, and my head ached from trying to remember the names of all my new teachers and classmates. As I shut my locker door for the last time, all I could think about was how much I just wanted to go home and forget this whole day had ever happened.

Then I spotted Addie at her locker. She was all alone, and she seemed to be having trouble opening the lock. I took a deep breath. Addie was my friend and I wasn't going to abandon her. "Hey, can I help you with that?" I asked, coming to her rescue. "I'm pretty good with them, like I told you this morning. Just tell me your combination and –"

"My combination is supposed to be secret, Jenny," Addie reminded me.

"Yeah, but it's just me," I said. "And I would never tell."

"It's okay. I'll get it," Addie assured me. "I should practice, anyway."

I nodded. "So, um, you want to come over after school today?" I asked her. "I want to hear all about your summer. And I know Cody and Sam are anxious to see you. I think they really missed you."

Addie rolled her eyes. "Mice don't miss people, Jenny."

"Sure they do," I said. "You should have seen how excited they were when I got home from camp. They came running over to the side of the cage."

"Oh, that's nice," Addie replied absentmindedly.

"So, can you?" I asked her.

"Can I what?"

"Come over after school."

Addie shook her head. "I have plans with Dana. We're going school supply shopping at the mall."

First lunch and now shopping? Since when were Addie and Dana Harrison such good friends? They hadn't even had one playdate the whole time we were in elementary school. We both thought she was kind of stuck-up, actually.

Then I remembered that they'd both spent the summer at the community center day camp, and swimming on the swim club team.

Well, if Addie liked Dana, maybe I would, too. People changed, didn't they?

"So maybe I could come shopping with you guys," I suggested to Addie. "My mom could drive and take all three of us to the mall to get notebooks and stuff." *There.* Now Addie would invite me to come along, and we could all three be friends.

But Addie *didn't* invite me. She just looked around anxiously and pulled on her long, curly blond hair.

There it was. That awful silence. I wanted to ask Addie

why she was being so mean, but instead I just kept talking. Maybe I was just reading her wrong.

"So, um, what did you think of Ms. Jaffe?" I asked her finally, just to break the silence.

"She was okay," Addie replied. "Just not as funny as Ms. Strapp. She was a riot. Remember when she came in and did that rap song about adjectives last year?"

I giggled. Ms. Strapp had been our fifth grade teacher. She'd always been able to make even the most boring things – like grammar – seem hilarious. "What about the time she taught us all how to do those dances from when she was a kid, because 'dance' was a verb?"

Before long, Addie and I were laughing together, talking about old times. It was like nothing had changed.

Except for how she had treated me earlier.

"Addie, how come you didn't save me a seat at lunch?" I asked her finally.

Addie got quiet and looked at the ground. "I was sitting with some of my other friends," she said plainly.

"But we always sit together at lunch."

"I know we used to," Addie admitted. "But I wanted to sit with my friends from the swim team."

"But aren't we friends?" I asked her.

"Sure," Addie said. And she didn't sound like she was lying or anything. "But we don't have to do everything together, you know. This is middle school. Things are different."

Just then, Dana appeared at the end of the hall. She

waved at Addie. Addie smiled back. "Look, I gotta go. I'll see ya later, okay?" Addie told me.

I watched as Addie ran off to go shopping with Dana, and not me.

Addie wasn't kidding. Things were different.

Suddenly, a tall thin girl in long cargo shorts and a tank top came up beside me. "Hey, aren't you in my English class?" she asked in a voice so loud it echoed through the nearly empty hallway.

I looked at her for a minute, surprised. Then I nodded. "I think so," I said quietly. "Ms. Jaffe. First period, right?"

"Ms. Jaffe's kind of boring, huh?" the girl said. "I almost fell asleep today when she was explaining how she wanted us to set up our notebooks."

"That was kind of boring," I agreed.

"My name's Chloe," the girl said. "What's yours?"

"Jenny."

"Cool. So, I guess I'll see you tomorrow."

I smiled at Chloe. The first real smile I could remember giving anybody all day. I was really glad that someone was finally being nice to me. "You bet," I told Chloe. "First period. I'll be there."

"Hi, honey. How was your first day in middle school?" my mom eagerly greeted me as soon as I walked through the door.

"Fine," I grumbled.

"Tough teachers?" Mom wondered.

I shook my head. "Nah. They're okay."

"Did you make any new friends?"

I thought about Chloe, but a twenty-second conversation did not count as friendship.

"Not yet."

"Do you have classes with Addie or any of your old friends?"

"I have English and gym with Addie, but I didn't see Felicia or Rachel at all today."

"Oh." She studied my face for a moment. "Are you okay? Did something happen?"

"It's just . . . forget it. You wouldn't understand." I really didn't want to talk about this anymore. I just wanted to go up to my room to be alone.

"Okay, well, whenever you want to go school supply shopping, let me know," she said, changing the subject. My mom's pretty good about letting things drop. "Do you have a list of the things you need?"

"I just need to check a few things before we go," I said.

"No problem, but I only have time for a quick trip. Any big stuff will have to wait until the weekend, okay?"

I scowled as I made my way up the blue-carpeted stairs to my room. Then I shut my bedroom and flopped down on the red-and-white gingham comforter on my bed. There was something kind of soothing about being in my room. It had looked this way for as long as I could remember. Yellow furniture, red carpet, red-and-white gingham comforter and curtains. Nothing ever changed in my room.

It would be nice if everything in the world was like that, too.

At the sound of the door opening and closing, my two white mice, Cody and Sam, began squeaking wildly. "At least you guys are glad to see me," I said as I pulled two mouse treats from the container near the cage. "No one else was today. I just don't get it." I took Cody from the cage and held him close as I stroked his soft white fur. "Addie was so mean to me. She's never acted like that before."

Cody snuggled in against my Camp Kendale T-shirt and gnawed happily on his treat. I looked down at him for a moment, and then it hit me. The T-shirt! That had to be it. Addie and Dana had been all dressed up today in cute tops and low-slung jeans. They had fit right in with seventh graders.

But not me. I hadn't been dressed like a seventh grader at all. Actually, I didn't look any different than I had in fifth grade. No wonder Addie didn't want me sitting with her at lunch. She didn't want the older kids to think her best friend was a little kid.

Suddenly, I felt a lot better. Once I understood what was probably going on in Addie's mind I could forgive her. In fact, I could do better than that. I could help her. From now on, I was going to have to act and look more grown-up, so that Addie wouldn't have to choose between me and the seventh graders anymore.

A bright smile formed on my lips as I placed Cody back in his cage and raced over to my computer. I logged on and quickly Googled the words "teen fashions." Almost instantly a huge list of websites appeared on the screen.

I scanned the names of the websites and saw www.middleschoolsurvival.com

Hmm . . . that sounded like what I was looking for.

I clicked on the site and immediately saw links for quizzes and advice columns. There were also tons of photos.

Instantly, I clicked on the section called "Fierce Fashions." Pictures of low-slung jeans, funky hats, and boots appeared. They were awesome. Just the kinds of things Addie and her new friends had been wearing today.

I hit the PRINT button on my computer, and pictures of really cool clothes began shooting out of the printer.

I smiled to myself as I stared at the photos. It looked like I'd be adding a few extra things to my school supply shopping list!

Chapter FOUR

IT'S NOT EASY finding different places to hide and eat your lunch. But that's what I had to do the whole first week of school. Tuesday the stairwell. Wednesday the library. Thursday the hallway near Mr. Collins's supply closet. Friday I was back to the phone booth.

It didn't exactly make for the perfect school dining experience. But I'd had no choice since I couldn't go clothes shopping until the weekend.

But when Monday came, I was ready to rock! "Oh, yeah," I murmured excitedly to myself as I headed to the school entrance for my second week in sixth grade. Things were already starting to look up.

To begin with, I already knew where all my classes were located so I wouldn't have to ask directions again. And some of the kids' faces were already beginning to look familiar. As I walked up the steps toward the school, I spotted two other sixth graders who had been in my math and Spanish classes. They smiled at me and I smiled back. A connection. Cool. And I hadn't even gone inside the school building yet.

I reached down and patted the pocket of my new jeans.

The five-dollar bill was still there. Dana had been right. A bag lunch was sooooo elementary school.

As I walked down the hallway of C Wing I felt *transformed*, mostly because of what I was wearing. My new outfit totally rocked. Somehow I'd been able to convince my mom that things like a newsboy cap, low-slung ripped jeans, and cowboy boots were every bit as important for school as a binder and pencils. And believe me, that hadn't been easy.

As I walked down the hallway toward my locker, I could feel the eyes of some of the other kids on me. My makeover was definitely working. I looked every bit as cool as the other kids now. Maybe even cooler. Now Addie wouldn't have to choose between her new friends and me.

As I headed down the hall, I saw Addie with Claire and Dana. They seemed to be having a very intense conversation. I reached out my arm just high enough so that when I waved to Addie, my new lemon yellow tank top scooted up just above my belly button.

But Addie, Dana, and Claire didn't wave back. Instead, they remained clustered together, giggling wildly about something.

"Check out the granny panties," Claire said, giggling. "Why would anyone wear them with low-slung jeans? You can totally see her Fruit of the Loomies."

"She's walking all bowlegged, like she's been riding a horse too long," Dana added with a laugh.

Addie giggled.

I looked around to see who they were talking about, but it was hard to tell who it could be. I didn't see anyone who was walking bowlegged or wearing Fruit of the Loom underwear.

For a minute I wondered if maybe they were talking about me. But I knew that couldn't be it. For one thing, I looked too cool. And for another, Addie would never let anyone make fun of me.

At least I didn't think she would.

"Hi, Addie," I said, as I came closer. "What's up, Dana? Claire?"

Dana and Claire looked at each other.

"Uh, hi," Dana said.

"Yeah. Um, hi," Claire added.

They looked at each other again. "We'll . . . uh . . . we'll see you later, Ad," Claire said. "Gotta go."

"Bye," I said, as they walked away. I was glad to see them go. Now it was just me and Addie.

"So, I went shopping this weekend, and got a bunch of new clothes," I said, pointing to the gray cap on my head.

"I noticed," Addie said.

"So, now we both have cool tees and new jeans," I pointed out to her. "Awesome, huh?"

Addie looked at my new clothes. "Well, it's not like we're wearing the same outfit or anything, Jenny," she pointed out. "And everyone gets new school clothes in September."

"Yeah, that's the best part of the new school year," I said. "Getting new clothes. I think half of the school was in Green Oz on Saturday." I purposely let Addie know that I had been shopping in Green Oz. Addie and I had always wanted to shop there, but our moms had always said the clothes were too grown-up for us.

Not anymore!

"Oh, Green Oz," Addie said. "That's a nice store, I guess. Dana and I like Rosie's better, though. It's got much cooler stuff. You should check it out sometime."

I sighed. Once again I had been just one step behind Addie and Dana on the coolness meter. At least Addie had told me about Rosie's having better stuff. Next time I would shop there. I smiled at her gratefully. "Thanks for the tip," I said.

Addie shrugged. "Sure. I gotta run. See ya later, okay?"

"Yeah," I said. "Maybe at . . ."

I was going to say maybe at lunch, but I never got to finish my sentence. Addie was gone before I could. I took that as a hint that she wouldn't be saving a seat for me at her table today.

I'd been dreading the fifth period bell all morning. In fact, for the first time in my life I was actually praying that science class would go on forever. I figured it was better to face the basics of how electricity works than to start another week facing the crowds of unfriendly faces in the cafeteria.

But all the wishes and prayers in the world can't stop the clock from turning, and before I knew what was happening that bell rang.

As I walked into the cafeteria, I made a point of not looking toward Addie's table in the back of the room. Instead, I hurried over to the lunch line and looked at my choices: bagels with butter, turkey sandwiches, pasta with tomato sauce, and some sort of brownish mystery-meat. It all looked really nasty and it smelled even worse. A brown bag lunch would be better than this. Finally I decided on the bagel – I figured that would be pretty hard for the cafeteria staff to mess up – a container of milk, and some red Jell-O. I paid my three dollars and took my tray.

Now came the hard part. Where was I supposed to sit? The stairwell? The library? Or maybe for something completely different, how about a stall in the girls' room?

"Hey, Jenny!"

Suddenly I heard someone screaming my name – *really screaming* – across the cafeteria. I blushed when I noticed how many people had stopped talking and turned to see what was going on.

But Chloe, the girl who had actually done all the yelling, didn't seem to be embarrassed at all.

"How ya doin'?" she asked as she caught up with me.

"Hi, Chloe," I answered quietly.

"So, are you sitting with anyone?" Chloe asked me, her voice still at top volume.

"I . . . um . . . well, not really. I don't know too many people in this school yet," I whispered.

Okay, that wasn't a hundred percent true. But the people in the school I did know either had lunch during another period or had ditched me. So it wasn't a complete lie, right?

"I know tons of people. My next-door neighbor, Marc, is in seventh grade and he kind of introduced me around," Chloe said. " I'm sitting with him, his friend Liza, and some kids from my old school. I went to Stevenson Elementary."

"I went to Washington Elementary School," I said.

"Oh, so you must live on the east side of town," Chloe said.

I nodded yes.

"No wonder I've never met you," Chloe continued. "Although I think maybe I saw you at the community center a couple of times."

"It's possible. I took pottery classes there last spring."

"Pottery. Cool," Chloe said. "So you wanna sit with us?"

I didn't have to think that over for too long. It wasn't like I had anyone else begging me to come sit with them. And besides, sitting with seventh graders would be kind of impressive. Addie wouldn't be the only one eating lunch with older kids.

"Sure," I said finally. "That'd be great."

I followed Chloe over to a table near the fruit-vending machines. Her friends looked up as we walked over.

"Hey, everybody, this is Jenny. She's stuck in Ms. Jaffe's English class with me. Jenny, this is everybody," Chloe introduced me.

A guy in a black vintage Led Zeppelin T-shirt laughed. "Very classy intros, Chloe," he said. "What's she supposed to call me? 'Every' or 'body'?"

I giggled. That one was actually kind of funny.

"So introduce *yourself*, big shot," Chloe told him, taking a huge bite of her turkey sandwich before she even sat down. "I'm hungry."

"Close your mouth, Chloe," one of two twins groaned.

"Ooh, gross," her sister added.

Chloe opened her mouth wide, and displayed her half-chewed food, her brown eyes laughing with delight.

"Okay, we're not all that nasty," the guy in the Zeppelin shirt told her. "I'm Marc."

"Hi," I said. "You're the one in the seventh grade, right?" I blushed the minute the words were out of my mouth. How stupid did *that* sound?

But Marc didn't seem to think it was stupid. "Yeah. I got here early and kind of scoped the place out before Chloe arrived."

"Hey, we were here last year, too, you know," one of the twins reminded him. She smiled at me. "I'm Marilyn."

"And I'm Carolyn," her sister added.

"You can tell us apart because I'm the cute one." Marilyn laughed.

"No, I am." Carolyn giggled.

I smiled. Considering both girls had the same long blond hair, small blue eyes, and rosy pudgy cheeks, any argument over who was the cutest seemed kind of ridiculous to me. If they weren't wearing different-color T-shirts, I doubt anyone would be able to tell them apart.

"And the genius over there, the one looking over his algebra textbook, is Josh. He's a total whiz," Chloe told me, pointing to her left at a dark-haired guy in wire-frame glasses and a black-and-white rugby shirt. "He's taking seventh grade math, even though he's just a puny sixth grader like us."

"Who are you calling puny?" Josh demanded. "I'm a black belt now, remember?"

"Sorry, Karate Kid," Chloe apologized sarcastically.

"Wow, do you really have a black belt in karate?" I asked Josh. Now that was impressive.

"It's actually in tae kwon do," Josh corrected her. "But I can never get Chloe to get it right."

"Whatever," Chloe replied with a shrug. "It's still a bunch of kicking, screaming, and breaking wood."

"I'd like to see you break a piece of wood," Josh shot back.

Chloe laughed. "No thanks. That's not my idea of a good time."

I turned to the only person who had not introduced herself. She was petite and had short brown hair that fell just below her ears. She'd been sitting there completely silent, watching us all with her intense brown eyes.

"And you are . . . ?" I asked her, amazed at how relaxed I had suddenly become in this new group of strangers.

"Liza," the girl replied so quietly that I could barely hear her. "I'm in seventh grade, too."

"Liza's the shy, mysterious type," Chloe said, obviously unaware that she was embarrassing Liza. Liza's face turned as pink as the stripes on her shirt. I knew just how she felt.

"So how come we didn't see you at lunch last week?" Marc asked me.

"Oh, I was here, but I had a lot of stuff to do. Like one day I had to make an important phone call, and another I had to go to the . . ."

"Yeah, I made the same phone call the first day I was in this place," Marc interrupted me with a knowing wink.

Now it was my turn to blush. Marc had obviously figured out my lunchtime secret. So much for seeming cool around seventh graders.

"Hey, it's okay," Marc told her. "The first week is always the worst."

I took a deep breath and let it out. He had no idea just how bad things had been.

"I like your hat," Liza interrupted shyly.

"Me, too," Chloe said. "It's the first thing I noticed when I got into English class this morning. Maybe I should get one."

Josh shook his head. "You don't need any help getting

noticed, Chloe," he assured her. "With that mouth of yours, you're hard to miss."

"Yeah, well, with that –" Chloe began.

"So, are you guys going to stay in your own classrooms this year?" Marc interrupted, turning the conversation to Marilyn and Carolyn in an obvious effort to stop an argument between Josh and Chloe before it started.

"What fun would that be?" Marilyn said. (At least I *thought* it was Marilyn. I couldn't remember which twin was in the green shirt and which was in the blue one.)

"Seriously. Why should I have to take a math test when she's so much better at math than I am?" Carolyn wondered.

"Yeah. But if I take your math tests, you've got to take my Spanish tests," Marilyn reminded her sister.

"No problemo," Carolyn replied.

"You two will get in big trouble if you get caught," Liza pointed out quietly.

"No one's caught us yet," Marilyn assured Liza. "Hey, even our mom gets us confused sometimes."

As everyone continued talking, my eyes sort of drifted off toward the windows. Addie and Dana were sitting there, whispering to each other, while Claire and Aaron blew the wrappers from their straws at each other, and Jeffrey seemed to be hurrying to finish some last-minute homework. It was pretty much the same kind of thing that was happening at our table, and yet somehow they seemed so much cooler.

"Forget about it, Jenny," Marc remarked from across the table.

"What?"

"I said forget about it," he repeated. "They never let anybody in. That group's set."

"Who?" I asked, embarrassed at having been caught staring. More blushing. *Great.*

Marc nodded over in the direction of Addie's table. "Those guys. The Pops."

"The *Pops*?"

"Yeah. 'Pop' as in popular. They're just a bunch of snobs who spend their whole lives trying to impress everybody. They're not really that great."

I shrugged. Deep down, I knew Marc was probably right. So how come I still really wanted to be one of them?

Chapter FIVE

MIDDLE SCHOOL RULE #3:

ANYONE WHO IS ANYONE AT
JOYCE KILMER MIDDLE SCHOOL
GOES TO THE CAFETERIA GIRLS' ROOM
AFTER LUNCH.

IT'S JUST THE THING TO DO. Or at least it's the thing the *Pops* do.

I found that out when I went there after lunch. There were like a hundred girls in the bathroom. Okay, maybe not a hundred, but you know what I mean.

Not that I had to wait for a stall or anything. I was the only girl in there who was actually using the bathroom. For everyone else it was just a place to talk about other people and put on makeup. Addie, Dana, and Claire were there giggling, and putting on layers of eye shadow, mascara, and lip gloss before their next classes.

As soon as I stepped out of the stall and walked over to the sink, Dana and Claire stopped talking. Ha! As if I'd really want to hear about some cute boy they spotted in the gym or who they were making fun of now.

Okay, I admit it. I probably would have really liked to have heard it. But there was no way I was going to let them know it! I just focused on the water flowing from the faucet and stared at the soap dispenser.

"Uh, nice boots," Dana said, barely trying to choke back a giggle.

"Thanks," I murmured.

"Value Shoe, right?" Dana asked.

"Huh?"

"I mean you got them at Value Shoe, didn't you?" Dana explained. "You must have. They're cheap copies of the designer boots my mother wears."

Ouch. Okay, that one hurt. There's nothing worse than being told you were dressed like somebody's mother!

Dana had definitely changed over the summer. Now she wasn't just boring – she was mean and boring!

"Of course, my mom's boots are made of a much better leather," Dana told Addie and Claire. "Those cheap imitations are so hard to walk in." She bent her legs slightly outward and pretended to walk like a cowboy with sore thighs.

I walked over to the paper-towel dispenser and wiped my hands, refusing to say anything more. I glanced over at Addie to see if maybe she would tell Dana to cut it out, but Addie seemed to be ignoring me all together. It was like she hadn't even heard the conversation.

And maybe she hadn't. She was incredibly focused on brushing some pale blue eye shadow on her eyelid.

I watched with amazement as an eighth grader walked over to talk to her.

"You're Addie Wilson, right?" she asked.

Addie nodded.

"I'm Sabrina Rosen," the eighth grader introduced herself. "I went to Washington Elementary."

"I remember," Addie replied. "You had Mr. Plotkin in fifth grade, right?"

Sabrina nodded. "Yeah. The one who spit when he talked. It was awful talking about space in science." She spit slightly when she said the word *space.*

Addie giggled, and Sabrina laughed along with her.

Now that was definitely impressive. Sabrina was an eighth grader, and yet, she had been the one to come over and talk to Addie. Not the other way around. That was huge!

Soon, Addie, Dana, and Claire were exchanging pots of eye shadow and blush with the older girls, bonding over their collections of Cover Girl, Hard Candy, and Jessica Simpson Dessert makeup. No one even seemed to notice I was there anymore. Not that I could have joined in on the conversation even if they had. The only thing I had that even remotely resembled makeup was a beeswax lip balm I'd bought at the drugstore.

I bumped into Chloe, Marc, and Liza again later in the day, while I was on my way to Spanish class. They were standing by the D wing lockers talking. Unlike Addie and her friends, these guys actually waved for me to come over and join the conversation.

"Hi, Jenny," Marc said, holding up a small video camera. "What's up?"

"What're you doing?" I asked him, turning away from the camera. I don't usually like having my picture taken, especially when I'm not ready for it. I always seem to wind up with a doofy grin on my face or something.

"I'm making a movie," Marc explained. "It's kind of like reality TV," Marc told me. "You know: 'What is it really like to go to Joyce Kilmer Middle School?'"

"Who'd watch that?" Chloe asked him. "School's boring."

"Not necessarily," Marc said. "You just have to know what to look for."

"Marc, turn off the camera, okay?" Liza asked him in her soft voice.

I smiled gratefully at Liza. It seemed like we had a lot in common – besides the blushing.

"Yeah, Jenny doesn't look like she's in the mood to be interviewed by *you*, Mr. Spielberg," Chloe teased him.

"Hey, don't make fun of Steven Spielberg," Marc warned.

"I wasn't," Chloe assured him. "I was making fun of you. And I was protecting Jenny." She turned to me and studied my face. "You don't look so good. Are you okay?"

No. I wasn't okay. Not by a long shot. My feet hurt from

walking up and down stairs all day in my new boots, and my head was hot from being under a hat. But I didn't say that. I didn't say anything at all.

"Oh, that was real nice of you, Chloe," Marc said, shaking his head.

Chloe frowned. "I didn't mean you don't look nice or anything, Jenny," she apologized. "I just meant your face was a little gray."

"Not much better, Chloe," Marc said, coming to my defense.

"Well, I'm just worried," Chloe continued. "She looked a lot better at lunch than she does now and –"

"Chloe," Marc interrupted her. "Quit while you're behind, will you?"

I had to laugh at that one. "I think I'm just tired," I told Chloe, letting her off the hook.

"Well, you'd better wake up," Chloe said. "We've got Spanish next. And I think we're getting our first vocabulary sheet."

"So soon?" I asked.

"Marc says señorita Gonzalez gets started right away," Chloe replied.

"*Sí,*" Marc agreed. "*Trabajamos mucho en la clase de español.*"

"Huh?" Liza, Chloe, and I all said at once.

"I said, there's a lot of work in Spanish class," Marc replied.

"Are you taking Spanish, too?" I asked Liza.

She shook her head. "French. I started last year, and I'm sticking with it."

Just then the bell rang.

"Okay, that's *adiós* for me," Marc said, moving away from the lockers. "I'm gonna be late for science." He turned to me before he left. "Let me know if you need any help with Spanish, okay?"

"Thanks," I said.

"De nada," he replied.

"Huh?"

"It means 'you're welcome.'" He held up his video camera. "Say bye to the camera."

I put my hand over the lens of his camera.

"Too late," he teased. "You're already part of the movie."

Great. So here I was, with a gray face, tired feet, and sweaty hair recorded for all time on camera. Just what I wanted.

As Marc walked away, I thought of something else they don't tell you in the school handbook. Beware of seventh graders who carry cameras.

Chapter SIX

"JENNY, I SAVED YOU A SEAT!" Felicia Liguori shouted as I climbed into the school bus at the end of the school day.

Seeing her at the end of the school day had really kept me going – especially since Addie and I hadn't been talking or sitting together on the bus, either. Talking to Felicia made it seem like everything was back to normal. No confusing halls, makeup parties in the bathroom, or girls making fun of my Fruit of the Loomies. Just Felicia and me riding the school bus together. Like the good old days.

"Check this out," Felicia said as I sat down.

Felicia opened her mouth wide, so I could see the thin metal band stretching over her front teeth. "I went to the orthodontist this weekend and got a retainer."

"Oh. Does it hurt?"

Felicia shook her head. "It's just kind of annoying. It makes it hard to talk."

She wasn't kidding. Suddenly all of Felicia's s's sounded like sh's.

"Are you gonna need braces?" Felicia asked me.

"Dr. Benton says he's not sure yet," I told her. "I still need to lose some more baby teeth." I frowned slightly. As if I hadn't felt like a baby enough these past two days, right?

But Felicia didn't make fun of my still having baby teeth. Instead, she started to laugh. "Oh, man, check that out," she whispered to me as Addie got on the bus.

"What?"

"Doesn't Addie look ridiculous?" Felicia said. "Rachel and I were talking about it at lunch. All that makeup and stuff. She's trying to look older, but I think she looks like a clown."

I stared at Felicia with surprise. Usually she was really kind to everyone. But that wasn't a nice thing to say at all. Especially since she and Addie had been friends for a long time, too.

"You were away all summer," Felicia continued in a low whisper. "You don't know what happened to Addie, do you?"

I leaned over closer so I could hear her better. I didn't want to miss a word.

"She and Dana are good swimmers," Felicia said. "And when they took the swim team test, they were really, really fast. So the coaches put them on the older team. The next thing you know Addie and Dana started getting really tight with all these seventh graders on the team. Addie stopped talking to Rachel and me, and started dressing like . . . like . . . that!" Felicia laughed. "She looks like how we looked when we got into my mom's makeup kit. Remember?"

I laughed at the thought of that. We'd looked pretty ridiculous with red lipstick all over our faces, and bright green eye shadow going from our eyelids all the way up to our foreheads.

"She puts all that makeup on at school so her mom won't find out," Felicia continued. "But she must have forgotten to take it off. Her mom's gonna kill her when she sees!"

I looked at Felicia strangely. She sounded like she was happy that Addie was going to get in trouble.

"Well, this is my stop," Felicia announced as the bus turned the corner. "Call me tonight?" she asked.

"Sure," I agreed. "Maybe we can do something this weekend, you, me, and Rachel."

"But not Addie," Felicia whispered.

I shook my head. No. *Not Addie.*

A few minutes later, the school bus stopped at the corner near my house. I walked down the stairs, and Addie followed close behind. I didn't even try to talk to her. I could take a hint.

But Addie hurried to catch up to me as we got off the bus.

"Hi, Jenny," she said.

"Hi," I answered, but not too nicely.

"What are you doing?"

"Walking home," I answered her.

"No, I mean this afternoon," Addie continued. "Do you have a pottery class or something?"

I shook my head. "It doesn't start for another week or so. I'm just going to do homework, I guess."

Addie nodded. "I have a lot of homework, too. Maybe we could do it together."

Huh? Now I was totally confused. We hadn't talked in days.

"I figure I haven't seen Cody and Sam in a while, and you and I haven't gotten a lot of time to talk since you got back . . ." Addie let her voice trail off.

And whose fault is that? I wanted to say. But I didn't. Addie sounded so much like her old self all of a sudden. I didn't want that to change, so I just answered, "Sure. You can come over."

"Great. We'll do homework together, and play with Sam and Cody," Addie said as she happily walked up the stairs toward my front porch. "But first, I've gotta use your bathroom."

When Addie walked out of the bathroom, the eye shadow, blush, mascara, and lip gloss were gone. She'd washed it all off. Now her mom would never know.

"So I guess you like middle school a lot," I said, walking over to Cody and Sam's cage and giving them their mouse treats.

"It's okay. I mean, it's still school."

"Yeah, but you have so many new friends and all." I picked up Sam and stroked his soft white fur.

Addie pulled Cody from the cage and began to pet his

back. "You've got a lotta friends, too," she said. "I saw you at lunch."

So Addie had been noticing me at lunch, too. Wow. I'd never even thought about that possibility.

"Anyway, it was pretty cool that Sabrina Rosen came over to talk to you in the bathroom today," I said.

"I guess," Addie said. "No big deal."

Those were the words that came out of her mouth. But the smile on her face let me know that Addie thought it was a *huge* deal.

For the first time since school began, I was starting to relax around Addie. Things seemed almost the way they'd used to. And yet, there was something really nagging at me. And the more I stared at Addie's clean face, the more I just had to ask her.

"Hey, Ad?"

"Yeah?"

"Can I ask you something?"

Addie shrugged. "Sure."

"Did you really come over here to hang out and do homework?"

"Why else would I come over?" Addie asked.

"I don't know. To wash your makeup off before your mom saw you with it?" I asked.

I regretted the words the minute they came out of my mouth. Addie turned white. She looked like I had just punched her in the stomach.

"I mean . . . I didn't mean, well, you know, I was just

wondering because . . . oh, never mind," I stammered nervously. "I know you wanted to see Cody and Sam."

Of course she did. She was cuddling Cody, wasn't she?

Addie nodded and petted Cody once more before gently placing him back in the cage. "I love your mice."

I smiled. Of course she did.

Addie asked, "Did you hear about the school dance next week?"

"I know – next Friday," I said, relieved that Addie had moved on to another topic. I was also happy to have known something before Addie did. "It was on the calendar in the back of the school handbook."

Addie giggled. "I can't believe you read that thing."

I blushed a little. "So, I guess you're going to the dance," I said.

She nodded. "Claire, Dana, and I are going shopping for new outfits on Saturday."

"Oh, that sounds fun," I said.

"Um . . . yeah. I guess," Addie murmured.

"I could probably use some new clothes, too," I suggested. "Does your mom have any more room in the car?"

Usually, I didn't like to invite myself somewhere. But Addie had brought it up. And she wouldn't have done that if she hadn't wanted me to come.

Addie shrugged. "Yeah, I guess. We're probably taking the minivan."

"Cool," I said excitedly. Then I stopped. I remembered I had said I would do something with Felicia and Rachel this weekend. But that was okay. I could shop with Addie on Saturday and hang out with them on Sunday or something.

"Oh, hi, girls."

Addie and I stopped talking when my mother appeared at my bedroom door. Not that we were saying anything too private. It just seemed weird to be talking about school stuff when my mom was around.

"It's great to see you, Addie," my mother continued. "It's been so long since you two have had a playdate."

I groaned slightly. I couldn't believe my mother had said that. *Playdate.* Even I knew that once you were in middle school you didn't call them that. I wasn't sure what you called what Addie and I were doing – hanging out, I guess – but it was *not* a playdate.

Luckily, Addie didn't seem upset at what my mother had said. "I know," she told my mother. "I've been crazy busy, with vacation and the start of school and all that."

"Well, I hope when things calm down, you'll come over more often. Maybe I'll take you two to the teddy bear factory store in the mall. I know you two love making those bears," my mother told her.

Oh, man. This was just getting worse and worse. Teddy bears? If Addie didn't think I was a baby before, she would now.

"Um, Mom," I said. "Addie and I are going to do some homework now. We have a lot of work. *Middle school* work."

"Oh, okay," my mother said sweetly. "Let me know if you two want a snack or something."

"Sorry about that," I said, as soon as the coast was clear.

"My mom's like that, too," Addie said. "She still thinks I want to go to the movies with her. Now why would I want to be seen at a movie theater with my mother?"

I looked at Addie with surprise. "Have you gone to the movies just with friends?" I asked her excitedly.

"Not yet," Addie admitted. "But soon . . . I hope."

I felt a little better. Maybe I wasn't as far behind Addie as I felt.

Addie didn't stay at my house long enough for us to get our homework done. We talked for a little longer, and then Addie went home. She said she had to make a few phone calls. *Probably to Claire and Dana*, I thought to myself as she left.

Still, maybe it was better to do homework alone. One thing I'd learned pretty quickly about middle school, the work is a whole lot harder. It wasn't the kind of stuff you could do with a friend – or even a semi-friend – in your room with you.

Semi-friend. I guess that's what Addie was to me now.

I sat down at the computer and tried to do my English homework, but I couldn't focus. I kept thinking about

Addie and if she came over just to wash off her makeup. How could you tell if someone was really your friend?

I thought about what my English teacher, Ms. Jaffe, had told us today about tests. She said they were a way to prove how much you knew.

That was it. A quiz. There were tons of them on that website I'd found the other day. Quickly I typed in www.middleschoolsurvival.com.

As soon as the website popped up, I searched the screen for the list of online quizzes. Finally, I found the one I wanted.

Is Your Friend Poison?

To find out, click the answer that best describes your friend. The results will follow.

If you told your friend a secret, what would she do?

A. Keep it to herself even if she was tortured by the enemy.
B. Try to keep the secret, but let it slip out by mistake.
C. Blab your deepest, darkest secret to the whole world just to make herself seem cool.

That was a tough one. Before the summer, I would have said A. But I wondered if Addie would tell Claire and Dana about all the stupid things my mom had said about play-dates and the teddy bear factory. Maybe they were laughing at me right now.

I decided to click B. It was sort of a compromise.

You and your pal are in the mall, trying on clothes. You put on an outfit that doesn't really look that great on you. Which is your friend most likely to do?

A. Say that you look nice, but you could look better, then offer to help you pick out something more suited to you.

B. Lie and say you look awesome so she doesn't hurt your feelings.
C. Let you buy the outfit, look awful, and then laugh at you behind your back.

Okay, that one was easy. Even though I didn't know for sure, I did suspect that maybe Addie's friends had been laughing at me in the hall. And although Addie hadn't exactly been laughing, she hadn't defended me, either. C was the answer.

When you're totally bummed out, does your best friend:

A. Come to your rescue and take you out for a good cry and a big banana split?
B. Steer clear and wait for you to come to her when you want to talk?
C. Ditch you for friends who won't be a drag on her mood?

I supposed the best answer to that question was probably B. Addie did talk to me today about school – and she even said she noticed that I had new friends, too. So she wasn't totally ignoring me. I guessed I could still come to her when I was upset – as long as I did it when Dana, Claire, and Jeffrey weren't around.

When you're out of school with a cold, what does your best friend do?

A. Bring your homework to your house, and give you all the buzz about what was going on at school.
B. Call you from her house to talk, so she doesn't get sick.
C. Hang out with someone else until you get better.

I read that one over and over again. I couldn't choose between B and C. I hoped Addie would at least call me if I were sick with the flu or the plague or something. But I couldn't be sure. Lately I wasn't sure of anything.

Your friend has made some new friends that you don't know. How does this affect your relationship?

A. It's so cool because now you've got a bunch of new pals, too.
B. You guys still hang out, just not as much because she spends some of the time hanging with the new crowd.
C. She drop-kicks your friendship right out the window.

Definitely B. Addie would never be seen with me in school. But at home, she was still sort of like the same old Addie.

I scrolled down for the results.

If you answered mostly A's, you can rest easy. Yours is a true-blue BFF. She'll be there for you through thick and thin.

If you answered mostly B's, it seems your friend is not the sweet, kind person she appears to be. There are a few dangerous aspects to her personality. No one's saying to steer clear of her completely, but it would be wise to keep your guard up.

If you answered mostly C's, dial 911 immediately and ask for poison control. This girl is toxic. Stay as far from her as possible.

Okay, that settled it. Addie wasn't exactly poison, but she wasn't my BFF, either. I was right. She was my semi-friend. Which I guess was better than her not being my friend at all.

Chapter SEVEN

WHEN I WOKE UP the next morning, I had made a decision. The next step toward getting Addie back would be putting on makeup in the girl's bathroom, just like Addie and the other Pops did. That would be a good thing.

The only trouble was, I didn't really know that much about putting on makeup. Addie seemed to know exactly what colors to use, and just how to put it on. Somehow she'd learned all that over the summer.

But I didn't have any friends who could teach me about putting on makeup.

On the other hand, I did have something else. A computer. Maybe middleschoolsurvival.com had some ideas about makeup.

My mom and dad wouldn't be awake for another half hour. That gave me just enough time to check the site. Quickly, I flicked on the computer and clicked on www.middleschoolsurvival.com. It was on my bookmark list now.

Sure enough, there's a link to "Makeover Madness." I double-clicked the mouse. Almost immediately, a whole group of topics appeared on the screen. I went right to

Eye-Deal

Eye Shadow Tips

Looking for the perfect shade of shadow for your eyes? Just follow these simple rules and you can't go wrong.

BLUE-EYED BABES: Brown and rose eye shadows were made for you. Apply the eye shadow from lash lines to the creases in your eyelids. Then top it with some dark brown or black mascara.

BROWN-EYED BEAUTIES: Green and gold are the colors for you. These shades will pick up the tiny colored flecks that are often found in brown eyes. Choose a shadow with just a little bit of shimmer, and apply the green shadow from the lash lines to the crease in your eyelids. Then add a pale cream color from the crease to your eyebrow. Finish it up with brown mascara.

GREEN-EYED GALS: Go for lavender and mocha shadows. Warm mocha is the perfect color for day wear, lavender will give you a purply glow for nighttime. Either way, remember to finish off your eyes with brown mascara.

HAZEL-EYED HONEYS: Deep green and pale yellow are the shadows for you. Choose a shadow shade that matches different flecks in your eyes. For added fun, apply your eye shadow, then line eyes with the same color, using a liner brush dipped in water.

I hurried into the bathroom and found my mom's makeup bag. Well, actually I opened one of my mother's many makeup bags. My mom has tons of makeup. Most of it is little samples she gets at the mall. So she's got tons of colors.

I dug through the bag until I found a pretty shade of lavender eye shadow and some brown mascara – everything the website recommended for my green eyes. Then I grabbed one of her old blushes, and a really pretty pink lipstick. Then I closed up the bag and went back to my room.

I smiled to myself as I placed the makeup in my backpack. My journey to the top of the Pops had definitely begun.

But I wasn't feeling that confident when I walked into first period English class that morning. In fact, I was a nervous wreck. My stomach was bouncing all around. It was like waves crashing up and down in there. *Tidal* waves. *Tsunamis.*

I guess I was nervous because both Addie and Chloe were in my English class. At school, I was getting friendly with Chloe – at least I'd felt that way at lunch yesterday. But Addie and I were friends, too – at home, anyhow. So it was sort of like my two worlds were colliding.

"Yo, Jenny, I saved you a seat," Chloe shouted the minute I entered the room. "Over here."

I looked over to the back of the room where Addie and Dana were sitting. They were looking at some pictures on Dana's camera phone. They didn't even glance up when Chloe called my name.

A camera phone. Wow. Dana was really lucky. I'd practically had to beg my parents to let me have a regular cell phone. And now that I had one they wouldn't let me even bring it to school. It was just to use at night or on weekends.

"And this is a picture of my sister and me at the mall," I heard Dana tell Addie. "Her friend took it."

"Where was your mom?" Addie asked.

"She just dropped us off. My sister and I go to the mall by ourselves all the time."

I nodded to myself. Now I knew why Addie so desperately wanted to go to the movies without a grown-up. It was a Pop thing.

I wondered if Addie's mother would be hanging out with us when we all went to the mall together this Saturday to shop for the dance.

"Jenny, didn't you hear me?" Chloe shouted again from her seat in the middle of the room.

Of course I heard her. Everyone in the room had heard her. People in Timbuktu had probably heard her.

"Uh, yeah. Sorry," I said as I slipped into the seat beside her. "I guess I was daydreaming."

"Cool sneakers," Chloe said, looking down at my red-and-white canvas Converses.

"Thanks," I murmured. I actually wasn't wearing the sneakers because they were cool. I was wearing them because my feet still hurt from those boots yesterday.

I looked down at Chloe's feet. She was wearing a really old pair of pink-and-white sneakers. Chloe didn't seem at all hung up on things like expensive shoes or clothes, either. At the moment she was wearing a pair of regular jeans that weren't low-slung or anything. Her T-shirt had a picture of a frog on it. It said HOP TO IT.

"So, did you get to see *Hot New Star* last night?" I overheard Addie saying to Dana. "That girl with the short blond hair can really sing."

"Amanda," Dana replied, giving her name. "She rocks. But I just watch for that judge from England. I think he's so cute."

"I know," Addie agreed. "English accents are so awesome. No matter who you are, if you talk with a British accent you're automatically cool."

"And smart," Dana added. "English people always sound so smart."

I had to agree with that. I wished I had watched *Hot New Star* last night. Then I could join in the conversation. But I'm not allowed to watch TV on school nights. My parents record *Hot New Star*, and I watch it on the weekends. But by then, it would be too late for me to talk about that with Addie and Dana.

When the teacher came in, the class grew quiet. Addie and Dana stopped talking. But they managed to keep up their conversation throughout the rest of class by passing notes. I watched as Dana scribbled something on a piece of paper, folded it up small, and then quietly dropped it on the corner of Addie's desk.

MIDDLE SCHOOL RULE #4:

PASSING NOTES IS COOL.

"Jenny. Jenny. Hello. Earth to Jenny McAfee!"

I jumped as I heard Ms. Jaffe call out my name.

"Um . . . here," I said quickly.

"I know you're here," Ms. Jaffe said with a deep sigh. "I'm not taking attendance. I just asked you if you could explain what an epic poem was."

I could feel my face turning red. The kids in the class were all laughing at me. Addie and Dana were giggling harder than anyone else. This day was starting out terribly.

So what else was new?

I had done my homework. I knew what an epic poem

was. I really did. But I couldn't seem to get the words out. Instead, I shrunk down in my chair. And I didn't say another word the entire morning.

I sat with Chloe and her friends at lunchtime, but I barely ate anything. I was too excited. I had a plan to put into action.

I kept one eye on Addie's table as I talked to my new friends. The minute I saw Addie, Dana, and Claire head into the bathroom, I grabbed my book bag, too.

"I . . . uh . . . I gotta go," I excused myself to my new friends.

"Where are you rushing to?" Chloe asked me curiously.

"Uh, the bathroom," I told her.

"Wait a minute," Chloe said. "I'll go with you."

No. That was definitely not going to work.

"Uh, sorry. Can't wait," I told her as I grabbed my book bag and rushed off.

The bathroom was totally buzzing by the time I got there. I practically had to fight my way to one of the mirrors. But I got one. Right next to Claire. Addie was by a mirror closer to the windows.

"Hi," I said to her.

"Hi," Claire replied, without even looking in my direction as she applied shiny lip gloss to her lips.

"I guess you're here to put on makeup, too," I continued.

Claire rolled her eyes. *"Duh."*

"I have a really pretty lavender eye shadow, if you want it," I said. "Of course you have brown eyes, so a green shadow would probably work better, but . . ."

Just then, Dana peeked over my shoulder to look at my makeup selection. I moved to the side for a moment so she could get a better look. "You can borrow anything you want," I said, as I applied the lavender shadow and topped it off with black mascara, just like it said on middleschool-survival.com.

"Why would I want to borrow this stuff?" Dana asked me. She picked up the pink lipstick. "Look, she's wearing Landfield. My *grandmother* wears Landfield."

"Mine, too." Sabrina laughed.

I bit my lip and tried not to cry. Tears would smear the black mascara I had just put on. "Well, maybe you can help me get some better stuff when we all go to the mall on Saturday," I suggested to Dana, as I put some blush on my cheeks.

Dana stared at me. "*You're* going with us? Yeah, right."

"I am," I told her.

"Says who?" Dana asked.

I looked over at Addie, hoping she would back me up. After all, she was the one who'd invited me.

"Oh, Addie, you didn't . . ." Claire began.

"All I said was my mom had room in the van for one more person," Addie insisted. "I never said she was invited. . . ."

I gasped. Suddenly I felt as though I couldn't breathe. The room was spinning all around. Sure, that *was* all Addie had said. But she'd meant I could come. I knew she had. And she knew it, too. But now, in front of her friends . . .

"Oh, man, nice cheeks." Claire giggled, looking over at me. "What are you going for, that circus look?"

I looked into the mirror. She was right. The blush I had taken from my mom's bag was way too red for my face.

"Come on, you guys, let's just go," Addie said.

I stared at the floor as Dana and Claire followed Addie out of the bathroom. One by one, the other Pops made their way out of the room, too.

"I can't believe she thought she was going to the mall with us." I heard Dana laugh as she walked away.

"Like that was going to ever happen," Claire added. "Boy, Addie, you've really got to watch what you say around her."

As the door slammed shut, I could feel the tears falling down my face. I could just imagine the black stripes dripping down.

So much for my brilliant plan. I looked ridiculous. I'd definitely made a fool of myself in front of all those popular girls.

But worse than that, *Addie* had made me look like an idiot. Or at the very least, she hadn't helped me *not* look like an idiot.

This day could not get any worse.

As I bent down toward the sink to wash the makeup from my face, I heard the sixth period bell ring. It was about to get worse. I was going to be late for Spanish, which meant I would have to do an extra homework assignment tonight.

"Middle school stinks!" I shouted out into the empty bathroom.

Chapter EIGHT

THE NOTE LANDED ON MY DESK at the exact moment señorita Gonzalez turned her back to write on the board. I grabbed it quickly, before anyone could see it, and opened it beneath my desk.

You want to play basketball with Marc and me on Saturday? He has a hoop in his driveway.
—C

That sounded great, but I had one problem with Chloe's invitation. I'd already made plans with Felicia and Rachel. But we hadn't decided what to do yet. That gave me an idea.

I sort of have plans with two friends from my old school. Can they come, too?
—J

I reached over my shoulder and passed the note back to Chloe. Not two seconds later, the paper was back on my desk.

Sure. The more the merrier. And wait until you taste Marc's mom's lemonade. It's da bomb!

I giggled slightly as I read the note. But I stopped laughing as soon as señorita Gonzalez turned back around. There was no way I would be able to explain why I was laughing without getting in trouble. Somehow I didn't think she'd believe that I found the numbers one through twenty in Spanish all that funny.

I looked down at the note again. The more the merrier. That was so cool. Definitely not the way Addie and her friends thought. They didn't want to let anyone else in on their plans. It was just those few special people. The Pops.

Which really didn't make all that much sense when you thought about it. If Addie and Dana and the rest of their clique were supposed to be so popular, how come there were so few of them? Didn't being "popular" mean that you were liked by everyone? But that wasn't how it was at all.

Now that I thought about it, I had a lot more friends than Addie did. There was the whole crowd Chloe had introduced me to. And I was still friends with Felicia and Rachel. And we weren't snobs. We would hang out with anyone who was fun. But we stayed away from the kids who had fun making fun – of other people, that is.

But I still wondered, if any of us got a chance to be a Pop, would we take it?

"Hi, Felicia," I said as she got on the bus that afternoon. "I saved you a seat."

Felicia hopped into the seat next to me and sighed heavily. "You wouldn't believe how much homework I have! It's scary."

"I know," I agreed. "I have a Spanish test coming up on Monday, and it's only the second week of school."

"I wish I was back in elementary," Felicia groaned.

If Felicia had said that earlier in the day, I would have totally agreed with her. But right now I was in such a good mood I couldn't. "I don't know about that," I said. "Who wants to eat lunch with their teacher?"

"Good call," Felicia admitted.

"And weren't you getting sick of the same thirty kids?" I continued. "It's so much better when you can meet new people."

I stopped for a minute, realizing what I had just said. What a difference a few days made.

"Have you met a lot of people?" Felicia asked. "Rachel and I really haven't."

Maybe that was because Rachel and Felicia didn't really have to go out and make a bunch of new friends. They had each other to eat lunch and hang around with.

But not me. I *had* to meet other people. Addie had shut me out completely.

"Some of my new friends are playing basketball on Saturday," I told Felicia. "You and Rachel want to come? That way you can meet everyone and shoot hoops."

"Your friends won't mind?" Felicia asked.

I shook my head. "They're – I mean *we're* – not like that."

All Thursday and Friday I tried hard to stay away from Addie and her friends. But it wasn't easy. Addie and Dana had the same English and gym periods as I did, so I had to see them, then. And of course, Addie was on my bus. But even though I knew I was angry with Addie for being such a jerk about the trip to the mall, I couldn't help missing her. We'd been friends for a really long time. You don't just turn that off like a light switch, you know?

The only thing that kept me going was the fact that I knew that I had plans this weekend. Addie might have thought she'd ruined my life by ditching me when she went to the mall with Claire and Dana, but she hadn't. There's more to life than shopping at the mall. Like basketball, for instance.

Chapter NINE

"SHE JUMPS. SHE SHOOTS. She . . . misses!" Marc shouted as he filmed Chloe shooting the ball at the hoop that hung over his garage door.

"Hey, big shot, if you think it's so easy, why don't you put down the camera and shoot a few?" Chloe playfully snapped back, sticking her tongue out at Marc.

"Here, Jenny, take this and tape me," Marc said, handing me his camera. "I want this recorded for all time. All you have to do is push the button until the red light goes on in the corner."

"You got it," I said, pointing the lens in his direction and catching every second of his dribbling, shooting, and – *swish* – sinking the ball right into the basket.

"Yeah, well, you're the one with the basketball hoop at your house," Chloe reminded him. "That sort of gives you an advantage."

As Marc and Chloe argued about whether or not that really was an advantage or if Marc was just a better athlete, I turned the camera toward Felicia. She'd gotten her hands on the ball and was dribbling toward the basket. Josh had his hands up and was trying to block her.

But it was no use. A whole summer of basketball camp

at the community center had trained Felicia well. She shot right over Josh, and sunk the ball into the basket.

"Josh, don't give up the karate," Chloe joked.

"It's tae kwon do," Josh replied. But he didn't really sound all that annoyed. Instead, he flopped down on the grass and wiped his forehead with the bottom of his shirt. "Man, it's hot out here," he groaned.

"Yeah, it's so hot the birds have to use potholders to pull worms out of the ground," Rachel joked.

"Ouch. That one was awful," I told her. But I laughed anyway. I was used to Rachel's bad jokes.

"Then how about, it's so hot you have to eat chili peppers to cool your mouth off," Rachel tried.

Chloe scowled at that one. "It doesn't seem fair that there should be school when it still feels like summer," she said, obviously trying to turn the attention away from Rachel and her jokes.

"It *is* still summer," Josh corrected her. "Until September twenty-first."

Felicia was still standing by the basketball court. "Hey, Rache," she called out. "Wanna shoot a few more?"

Rachel shook her head. "This game's been canceled on account of sweat," she told her.

Marc wiped a few beads of sweat from his forehead and then started to walk toward the side of his house.

"Where are you going?" Josh asked him.

"Be right back," Marc assured us with a chuckle.

"I don't like the sound of that," Chloe said.

I looked at her strangely. What was the big deal about Marc going around to the side of his house?

Chloe definitely knew her next-door neighbor a whole lot better than the rest of us. Sure enough, Marc was up to no good. A moment later he returned. And instead of holding his camera in his hand, he was holding the garden hose.

"GOTCHA!" he shouted out, spraying us all with icy-cold water.

The first shock of the water was awful. It was freezing. But after a few seconds, we were all happy to be jumping around in the spray.

Still, it didn't seem fair that Marc could get us, when we couldn't get him back. And since he had the hose, there could be no element of surprise. Unless . . .

Suddenly a plan hatched in my brain. "I'm gonna get Chloe," I whispered to Marc as I grabbed the empty bucket from near the side of the house.

He smiled mischievously. "Go for it," he whispered back, filling the bucket to the brim with icy water.

I pretended to race over toward Chloe. But at the last minute, I turned back and dumped the whole bucket of icy-cold water right on Marc's head.

"Oh, that's it, J," Marc shouted. He pointed the hose at me. I tried to run, but it was impossible to escape the stream of water that was flying in my direction.

By the time my mother arrived to take Felicia, Rachel, and me home, I was soaking wet. And so was everyone else. We were all sitting on the grass, sipping cold lemonade.

"Boy, I'm glad I didn't bring the car," my mother said, laughing as she walked up onto the lawn. "You two would have destroyed the seats."

At that moment, all the joy washed out of my face. "What do you mean you didn't bring the car?"

"It's a nice day. I figured we could walk. We'll cut through the park," my mom explained.

"Cool. Can we get an ice cream on the way?" Felicia didn't seem to have any problem with that, but I sure did.

"Sure," my mom agreed.

"Awesome. Thanks, Mrs. McAfee," Rachel added.

I looked at Felicia and Rachel with amazement. Didn't they get it? My mother was walking us home – like we were babies or something. What if we ran into Addie or Dana along the way?

I watched as my mom and Marc's mother introduced themselves and spoke for a few minutes. Then, as my mom turned to leave, I thanked Mrs. Newman for having me over.

"I see Marc hasn't beaten those manners out of you yet," Mrs. Newman told me with a grin.

"Give me time," Marc called over to her.

"Leave Jenny alone. I love nice manners," Mrs. Newman said.

My mother smiled proudly at that. You know how it is with parents. Whenever you get a compliment they act like it's for them or something.

"Well, we're off," my mother remarked finally.

"Bye, you guys," Chloe said.

"See you at school," Marc added.

"Yeah," Josh said. He smiled at all three of us, but the way he grinned at Felicia tipped us off that he liked her.

"Bye," she answered him in a kind of shy voice.

"Yeah. Bye," I added. Then I turned to Felicia and Rachel. "Race ya!" I shouted.

"Okay!" Felicia agreed excitedly.

"You're on," Rachel added.

As we took off down the street I smiled slightly. I figured if we ran far enough ahead of my mom, people would think we were really running home by ourselves.

Of course, that only lasted as far as the park. The minute my mother spotted the ice-cream stand, she called out to us. "Jenny, Rachel, Felicia, don't you want an ice cream?" she asked.

Rachel and Felicia stopped right away. Neither of them would ever give up a chance for an ice-cream cone. So I had to stop, too. I figured I might as well get a cherry Popsicle. I mean, it's not like I could race myself, right?

By some miracle, we managed to drop Felicia and Rachel at their houses without bumping into one person we knew from school. But as soon as my mom and I reached my neighborhood, we passed right by Addie, who was sitting on her front steps. She was wearing a cute little denim miniskirt and a white tank top. Her hair was pin straight, which was weird, because her hair is usually so curly.

I looked down at my old pink T-shirt, which was still sopping wet and now had a big red Popsicle stain on it. I knew my hair was a disaster, too – that's what happens when you have icy water sprayed right on your head.

"Hi, Addie," my mother called over to her. "How are you doing?"

Addie shrugged. "I wanted to go to the mall, but my mom is busy gardening."

I smiled to myself. So Addie and the Pops hadn't made it to the mall after all.

"Your mother's right. It's too nice out for you to be inside at the mall all day," my mother told Addie. "It's too bad Jenny didn't know you had no plans. You could have gone with her to play basketball and have a water fight at her friend Marc's house."

I gasped. I couldn't believe my mother. How could she have said something like that? But I guess that wasn't her fault. She thought Addie and I were still friends.

"Well, I just straightened my hair," Addie said slowly. "It took a long time. I don't know if I would have wanted to get it all wet."

"Your hair does look lovely," my mother assured her.

"But I guess it doesn't really matter," Addie continued. "It's just going to curl up in all this heat, anyway."

"True," my mom continued. "But there's nothing like a good water fight on a hot day." She started to walk down the block toward our street.

"Yeah," Addie said quietly.

For a second I got the feeling that she would have rather spent the morning shooting hoops and having a water fight than straightening her hair.

Not that Addie would ever admit being jealous of anything I'd done. Why should she? It's not like I would ever admit to anyone that I was jealous of Addie and the Pops, right?

"See you later," I mumbled to Addie as I followed my mom.

"Sure, later," Addie said.

Chapter TEN

WHEN THE PHONE RANG early on Sunday morning I knew it had to be for me. My parents' friends never call early on the weekends. They all know that my parents love to sleep in.

I hurried to get the phone on the first ring, so it wouldn't wake up my parents. "Hello?" I said.

"Hi, Jenny. It's me, Felicia."

"Hey. What's up?"

"I just wanted to say thanks for inviting Rachel and me yesterday," she said. "I really liked your friends."

"And they liked you," I said, thinking about Josh especially.

So was Felicia.

"Josh was nice," she said. "And he's so funny."

"Yeah, he is," I agreed. "And smart, too. He's taking seventh grade math."

"Wow." Felicia was really impressed.

"And I think he likes you," I added. I stopped for a minute and took a deep breath. I'd never had a conversation like this with anyone, ever.

"I wish there was some way I could find out if Josh *really* likes me," Felicia said hopefully.

"You want me to ask him?" I suggested.

"No. It would be too embarrassing," Felicia continued.

I glanced over at the computer against the wall, and thought about the friendship test I had tried the other day. "Maybe there's an online quiz you could take? I know this really great website. . . ."

"Oh," Felicia said with a little bit of disappointment. "I'll never get near the computer today. My sister has to write a paper for her history class."

"Oh, well, I could go online and read you the questions," I suggested. I never have to wait to use the computer at my house. It's one of the advantages of being an only child.

"Could you?" Felicia asked.

"Sure. Just give me a minute," I said as I turned the computer on, and went straight to middleschoolsurvival.com. "Here's one that looks right," I said. "It's called 'Does He Like You?' "

"Perfect!" Felicia exclaimed.

"Okay, first question," I said as I began to read the quiz.

Does he tend to think about your needs before his own?

- Yes
- No

Felicia thought about that for a moment. "Well, he did give me a glass of lemonade before he took one, and he was really thirsty."

"It's yes then," I said excitedly, as I clicked the button. A new question popped up on the screen.

Do you often catch him looking at you even when there are other things going on around him?

- Yes
- No

"I can answer that one," I said. "Definitely."

"Really?" Felicia asked. She sounded so happy.

"Oh, yeah," I said, clicking the YES button. The next question popped up.

Does he do things to catch your attention, even if it makes him look like a fool?

- Yes
- No

"I don't think Josh looked like a fool at all yesterday," Felicia said sadly. "So I guess that one is no."

"Oh, yeah? What about trying to guard against you in basketball? He's terrible at basketball. He just did that so he could hang out with you," I insisted, hitting the YES button without even asking Felicia if she agreed.

Does he always seem to be fixing his hair or clothes when he sees you?

- Yes
- No

"Okay, that one's a no," I admitted. "But it doesn't really count, because we were having a water fight and no one fixes their hair in a water fight."

"That's true," Felicia admitted, but she did sound kind of disappointed at having to give a no answer on the quiz.

When he's with his friends, does he spend more time talking to you than them?

- Yes
- No

"He played some one-on-one basketball with me," Felicia remembered. "But is that really talking? I mean, we didn't have a conversation or anything."

I didn't know how to answer that. "I won't click either button," I said, hitting the mouse so I could advance to the next part of the test. "Okay, now we're going to find out your results. You said yes to three out of five questions." I scanned the list to see what that meant.

5 out of 5 yes answers: Keep this boy away from banana peels. He's already fallen hard . . . for you!
4 out of 5 yes answers: This guy has definitely got you on the brain!
3 out of 5 yes answers: We sense the beginning of a beautiful friendship . . . or more. Only time will tell.

2 out of 5 yes answers: It's time to move on. There are plenty of fish in the sea – go buy a fishing rod.

1 or 0 yes answers: Fuggedaboutit! This guy's just not interested.

"A beautiful friendship, huh?" Felicia said, sounding disappointed.

"Or more," I corrected her. "It says only time will tell. And don't forget, we didn't really answer the last question. So you really got three out of four yeses."

"I guess." She paused for a minute. "Do you think Josh is going to the dance?"

"I could find out," I said. "Why? Are you?"

"Aren't you?" Felicia asked me.

I was quiet for a minute. I hadn't really thought about it. In fact, the only time the dance had ever come up in conversation was that day Addie came over. I guess I had assumed that it was just the Pops who went to stuff like that. Still, if Felicia was going, then maybe I would, too.

"I'm not sure yet," I said. Then I laughed. "Only time will tell."

"So, um, are you guys going to the dance?" I asked the next day as I sat down for lunch at my regular table. How cool was that? I had a regular table. With my own crowd of friends.

"I doubt it," Chloe said between bites of a baloney sandwich she'd brought from home. Apparently Chloe didn't think it was lame to bring your own lunch to school. As usual, she did whatever she wanted.

"Oh, come on," Marilyn said. "You have to come."

"Yeah," Carolyn agreed. "The dances are hilarious. You gotta see how those Pops get all dressed up . . . just to stand there and watch everyone else have a good time."

"I don't even pay attention to them," Marc said. "At most dances I end up playing Ping-Pong in the gym. They show a movie in the auditorium, too." He turned to Liza. "What movie did they show at the spring fling dance?"

"I think a bunch of stupid cartoons," Liza replied with a giggle.

"Totally G-rated," Marilyn added. "With no violence at all."

"The school's afraid of freaking out our parents," Carolyn suggested.

I smiled. I was glad I didn't have parents that freaked out too easily. My mom and dad might not let me go to the movies with my friends if there was no grown-up around, but at least they took me to good movies. Some of them were even PG-13, which was pretty cool since I was only eleven and a half.

"Yeah, but the Ping-Pong's fun, and the snacks aren't half bad. They had foot-long heroes at the last one," Marc told me.

"They were delicious," Carolyn recalled.

"So are you going to come, Jenny?" Liza asked me.

"Maybe we could go together. My big sister could drive us. She just got her license."

Wow! Liza had a sister who was old enough to drive. How cool was that? Still, I doubted my parents would let me get in a car with someone who had just learned how to drive.

"Maybe you could eat over at my house, and then my dad could drive us," I suggested, trying not to hurt her feelings. I figured it had taken a lot for her to ask me to go with her. She was so shy.

"Okay," Liza replied. "I'll ask my mom."

"So . . . um . . . are any of your other friends going to the dance?" Josh piped up nervously.

"You mean like *Felicia*," Chloe teased him.

Josh bit his lip. His cheeks turned redder than the tomato on his sandwich.

"I didn't mean anyone special," Josh murmured. "I just thought that Jenny might have friends from her old school, and you can never have enough friends."

"Yeah, right," Chloe said, laughing. "Whatever you say, Josh."

"I think Felicia and my friend Rachel are going to the dance." I glanced over at the Pops' table. I was pretty sure Addie and Dana would be at the dance, too. But I didn't say anything about that. After all, Josh had only asked about my *friends*.

"Oh, okay," Josh said, trying to sound like he didn't

notice I had said Felicia was going to the dance. He wasn't very successful. The smile on his face gave him away.

I couldn't wait to tell Felicia!

Bad news! I had gym sixth period, right after lunch, and the grilled cheese sandwich I'd eaten was stuck somewhere between my chest and my stomach, and it didn't seem to be moving. Chloe was smart to bring her own lunch. The school food was the worst!

But my undigested sandwich wasn't the worst part about gym. The worst part was that both Addie and Dana were in the class with me. That would be okay, if some of my friends were in there, too. But they weren't.

To make things worse, this was gym. It was one thing for Addie and Dana to sit near each other in English class, because they hardly got a chance to talk in there. But in gym class, kids can talk the whole time. And Dana and Addie sure did a lot of talking!

"Did you see what she was wearing today?" Dana chuckled as she and Addie walked out to the field together.

I gulped. Would they really talk about me when I was just two steps behind them? I guess it wasn't that big of a shock. They'd done it before.

"I know. Who puts on purple tie-dyed sweatpants to go to school?" Addie agreed. "Especially homemade ones."

Phew. Okay. So it wasn't me they were talking about. I was wearing jeans.

"She probably made them at the community center

this summer," Dana said. "Didn't she and Rachel have arts and crafts in the afternoons?"

She and Rachel. I frowned. I didn't get to see Felicia this morning because her mom drives her to school. But I'd bet anything she was the one in the tie-dyed sweatpants.

"And have you heard her talk lately?" Dana said. "You can't even understand her with that weird retainer in her mouth."

"I know," Addie said and giggled. "My name isch Felischia," she added, imitating her.

Now I was really mad. It had been one thing when Dana had been saying all the bad things and Addie had just been agreeing. But now Addie was being every bit as mean!

Addie had gone over to the dark side. She was lost forever!

"Well, at least she'll have straight teeth," I shouted at Addie. "Not fangs like you have coming out of the sides of your mouth!"

It was true. Addie had two teeth that were slightly longer than the others on either side of her mouth.

Addie and Dana stopped in their tracks, turned around, and stared at me.

"What did you say?" Addie demanded.

"You heard me."

Addie looked as though I had just punched her in the stomach. She was in shock. I think she found it impossible to believe that anyone would say anything like that to a Pop.

I couldn't believe I'd said it, either.

"Yeah, well, at least Addie doesn't eat lunch with the Geek Squad, the way you do, " Dana spat back. "I mean, that girl, Chloe? What a loudmouth. And those twins? What are their names? Tweedledum and Tweedledummer?"

"It's Marilyn and Carolyn," I informed her. "And they're really funny and interesting. So is Chloe, for that matter. She's a riot. At least she's got a personality. She talks about more than makeup and clothes. She's unique. Not like you clones!"

My heart was pumping really hard now. My stomach was all in knots. I knew that I had just ended any chance at being part of the Pops or being best friends with Addie again.

As I stared into Addie's glaring blue eyes, I knew one thing for sure.

This was war!

Chapter ELEVEN

"YOU KNOW WHAT, I think it's time we showed the Pops who the coolest kids in the school really are," I told Chloe and Felicia when I met up with them in the hall at the end of the school day. We were standing by Chloe's locker, which gave us a good view of the other end of the hall where Addie, Dana, and Claire were busy checking themselves out in the mirror that was attached to Addie's locker door.

"They *are* the coolest kids in the school," Felicia said.

"Oh, give me a break," I said angrily. "They just act that way. I think they're boring and stupid!"

Chloe and Felicia looked at me strangely.

"What brought all this on?" Chloe asked me.

"Um . . . nothing. I don't know. They just bug me," I said. I didn't want to tell them about the mean things Addie and Dana had said.

"I don't know why you even think about them," Chloe told me. "I never do. I just pretend they're not there."

"But doesn't it bother you that they walk around like they own this place?" I asked her. "That they have this tight little crowd and they don't let anyone else in?"

"Why would I want to be part of their crowd?" Felicia asked.

I didn't really have an answer to that. I had wanted to be a Pop, ever since the first day of school. But now, after hearing how mean Addie had become, I knew I could never be a Pop. Yeah, I had said some mean things to Addie, too, but that was in defense of my friends. I wasn't the kind of girl who liked making other people feel bad.

Which was why I couldn't tell Felicia and Chloe what Dana and Addie had said about them. It would just make them feel awful. And that wasn't who I was.

The next morning I made sure to sit as far from Addie and Dana as I could in English class. I figured they'd still be talking about me, especially since I was probably the only person in the history of the school to ever stand up to a Pop.

After English I didn't see Addie or Dana again until fifth period. So the morning sailed by pretty smoothly – I even managed to get a four out of five on my math quiz. So as I entered the cafeteria I was feeling really good about myself.

MIDDLE SCHOOL RULE #5:

NEVER FEEL TOO GOOD ABOUT YOURSELF. SOMEONE WILL MAKE IT THEIR BUSINESS TO KNOCK YOU DOWN AGAIN.

In this case, that person was none other than Addie herself. She was standing two people behind me in the lunch line.

"She's had those jeans for two years already," she was saying to Dana. "Look how short they are."

"I think she's expecting a flood," Dana giggled.

I knew they were talking about me. But they were wrong. My pants weren't too short. Not at all. They were just fine. And they weren't two years old, either. I'd only bought them last spring.

Anyway, I wasn't going to give Addie and Dana the satisfaction of getting all upset. I just stared straight ahead and put a container of milk on my tray.

"It's so funny that she actually thought we would take her to the mall with us," Dana continued.

"Like that was ever going to happen," Addie agreed.

I smiled to myself. I knew for a fact that they hadn't even gone to the mall.

"I think she really thinks you guys are still friends," Dana told Addie.

"Oh, please," Addie replied with a sigh. " We were only friends because our moms are friends. That's what happens in elementary school. But now I'm old enough to choose my own friends. And can you imagine me hanging out with a geek like her? Please!"

That was it. I couldn't take it anymore.

Everything that happened next is kind of a blur. All I

know is that I picked up a big cup of this purple yogurt stuff – they call it "fruit float" on the cafeteria menu – and hurled it at Addie. Purply goo oozed all over her super-straightened hair, and her brand-new blue-and-white peasant blouse.

"Are you nuts, Jenny?" Addie screamed in surprise. "This stuff stains. And I'm wearing a brand-new shirt. You are *so* dead!" She grabbed a container of fruit float and dumped it on my head.

Suddenly the fruit float was flying everywhere. Addie and I just kept throwing it, smearing it, and pushing each other into it. Dana moved out of the way – Addie may have been her new BFF, but she wasn't about to get fruit float in her hair.

My friends, however, had come racing over. They were cheering me on from the sidelines.

"Yeah! Go, Jenny!" I could hear Chloe shouting out over the rest of the noise. And then, Mr. Collins, the janitor, jumped between Addie and me. "Whoa. What's going on here?"

Addie and I just stood there for a minute, staring – no make that *glaring* – at each other.

"She started it," I said finally.

"No, you did," Addie shouted back. "You threw that whole big thing of fruit float at me."

"Only because you and Dana were saying horrible things about me."

"Well, it's all true," Addie responded.

“Okay,” Mr. Collins said. “That’s enough. I don’t care who started it. It’s finished right now. Do you girls have any idea what a mess you’ve made? It’s hard enough cleaning this cafeteria after lunch. Now I’ve got all this extra purple goop to clean up, as well.”

I frowned as I looked around. The place was kind of a mess now. It would take a while to clean up. Mr. Collins shouldn’t have had to clean all that up on his own.

Come to think of it, I was kind of a mess, too. I had fruit float in my hair, my pants, and even in my shoes. And it was starting to stink like spoiled milk.

“I’ll help you clean up,” I told Mr. Collins. And I meant it.

“You bet you will,” he replied, looking angrily at Addie and me. “You both will. And then we’ll see what other punishment the principal can come up with.”

“So how much trouble did you get in?” Chloe asked me that night on the phone.

“My parents were pretty mad,” I admitted. “I’m grounded for the whole week and I can only talk on the phone for a few minutes each night.”

“Oh, man, that stinks,” Chloe commiserated with me. “That means you can’t go to the dance.”

“Well, not exactly,” I said slowly. “I can go to the dance. I just can’t have any fun there.”

“Huh?” Chloe sounded confused.

“It’s part of the principal’s punishment. Addie and I have to spend all night serving snacks at the refreshment table.”

"Well, at least you'll be there," she said, trying to make me feel better. "And you'll get first dibs on the best food."

"I guess," I admitted.

"And you can save the best snacks for us," Chloe continued. "Just stick 'em under the table or something."

I giggled. "You got it," I assured her.

"That was pretty cool, what you did today," Chloe complimented me. "I couldn't believe you did that to that Pop girl."

"I told you yesterday I was getting sick of those Pops being jerks to everyone," I reminded her.

"Yeah. But everybody feels that way. You were the only one who did anything about it."

That was true. And despite the fact that I was in big trouble with my parents, I wasn't sorry about it at all.

"You're like a celebrity," Chloe gushed. "A legend. The first girl ever to cover a Pop with fruit float."

"Come on, Chloe," I said, pretending I wanted her to stop. But I really didn't.

"I'm telling you, this is going down in Joyce Kilmer Middle School history," Chloe assured me. "Marc says he got some great shots of you dumping that purple gunk all over Addie's head. You're the new hero in his film."

"A hero?" I repeated.

"Totally," Chloe agreed.

"Wow," I murmured. What more could I say?

* * *

When I walked into school on Wednesday morning, I knew everything had changed. Kids were smiling at me in the halls. Even eighth graders!

"Yo, Jenny! How are you?" an eighth grade girl with long red hair greeted me as I walked into C wing.

I stopped for a minute and looked at her with surprise. It was Sonia, one of the eighth graders who had sent me on a wild-goose chase for the elevators on the first day of school.

"Hello?" I said, more as a question than a greeting.

"Nice food fight," she complimented me. "You got that Pop big-time."

"Uh . . . thanks," I said. I turned to walk away.

"Hey, you're still not mad about that whole pool and elevator thing are you?" Sonia asked.

I shook my head no. I wasn't mad anymore. It seemed like it happened forever ago.

"'Cause it was just a joke," Sonia assured me. "We play it on all the sixth graders. But if we had known back then how cool you are . . ."

Whoa. Me? Cool?

"Well, anyway, see you at the dance," Sonia said. "You'll be there, won't you?"

I nodded. "I have to be. It's part of my punishment."

Sonia laughed. "Well, I'll see you there, 'kay?"

"Okay," I said. And as I walked away, all I could think was: Lizard Girl was gone for good. Long live Jenny . . . hero of the non-Pops!

Chapter TWELVE

SERVING PIZZA AND JUICE was definitely better than doing extra chores around the house. It was good to be out with other kids and listening to music, even if the dance wasn't exactly all I'd dreamed it would be.

"I can't believe the principal made you wear that." Rachel giggled as she walked up to the refreshment table with Marc. She was pointing at the hairnets Addie and I had been required to wear.

"I think it's cool," Marc teased. "We should all wear one. We could start a new fashion trend."

"Oh, yeah. That'll happen," I answered him.

"I think pizza is a great snack," Rachel said, taking a slice and changing the subject.

"Yeah, it's definitely better than anything they serve in the cafeteria during the day," Felicia added.

"But do you know where the best place to have pizza is?" Rachel asked.

"Where?" I wondered.

"In your mouth!" she declared with a grin as she took a huge bite of her slice.

"Oh man, Rachel, your jokes are getting worse," Felicia said. But she was laughing just like the rest of us.

All of my friends took turns visiting me at the table, which was more than I could say for Addie's crowd. They hadn't come over to the refreshment table once. The Pops were all too busy standing against the wall of the cafeteria in their new clothes. They weren't dancing or anything. They were just standing there, listening to the music, and acting bored.

Besides, I was pretty sure they didn't want to be seen around Addie while she was wearing a hairnet. You should have seen Addie's face when the principal handed her that net – she almost died. She'd spent at least an hour straightening her hair. And now she had to cover it up.

I glanced over at Addie and tried to smile. I actually felt kind of sorry for her. *But only for a minute.* You wouldn't believe the nasty look she gave me. Like I didn't have the right to look at her or anything.

"Hardly anyone's dancing," I noted, turning my attention back to my friends.

"No one ever does at these things. Maybe a few eighth grade girls, but that's about it," Marc said. "I told you. Everyone's either watching a movie or playing Ping-Pong and basketball."

"Or eating," Josh said, coming over to stand next to Felicia. "Can I have another slice, Jenny?"

"Sure." I put a fresh slice of pizza on a paper plate.

"I'm so hungry," Josh continued. "We've been playing basketball all night."

"He's really getting good," Felicia told me.

"Nah. You and Rachel slaughtered me," Josh admitted.

"But you're getting better," Felicia assured him.

"Definitely," Rachel agreed.

"You should see me in tae kwon do. That's when I really rock," Josh boasted.

"I'd love to see you do tae kwon do," Felicia said sincerely.

Josh grinned at her.

Wow. I could tell Josh and Felicia were getting along really, really well.

So could Addie. She was pretending like she didn't care enough to listen to our conversation, but she was. Addie was totally surprised that Felicia had someone who liked her, and *she* didn't!

"So you guys want to play basketball tomorrow at my house?" Marc asked everyone.

"Sorry, I can't," I said. "I'm grounded, remember?"

"Oh, yeah," Marc recalled.

"It's going to rain, anyway," Josh pointed out.

"Maybe we can all hang out at your house," Felicia suggested to me. "Watch a movie or something."

"I guess that would be okay," I said. "My folks said I had to stay home. But they didn't say I couldn't have anybody over to keep me company."

"Cool," Marc said. "I'll tell Chloe, Liza, and the twins."

As he walked off, I smiled to myself. There was going to be a whole crowd of kids hanging out in my house tomorrow. My friends. My *middle school* friends.

I looked over at Addie. She was standing all by herself pouring apple juice into little paper cups. She seemed miserable and lonely. *Just the way I'd looked on the first day of school.*

I guess being a Pop isn't always all it's cracked up to be.

Are Your Friends True Blue . . . or Just Using You?

It's a Friday night, and your pals all want to go to the movies. But you're totally grounded. What does your clique do?

A. Choose one representative to hang with you while the others hit the cineplex.
B. Go over to your house and rent a flick instead.
C. Go to the movies and leave you at home, but promise to hang with you when your grounding is up.

The most popular girl in school hates you. She vows to socially destroy anyone who is friendly with you. What do your friends do?

A. Take a stand and stick with you, willing to risk total social disaster.
B. Leave you all alone to fend for yourself.
C. Hang with you, but only when no one is watching.

You drop your tray in the lunchroom and spill spaghetti sauce all over your new shirt. What do your friends do?

A. Applaud and laugh with the rest of the kids in the caf.
B. Go to the bathroom with you and help you wash the red stuff off your shirt.
C. Hurry to their lockers to loan you anything they can find.

You spent Saturday night at a sleepover with a bunch of your friends. But now it's Sunday and you're totally not prepped for that big history test tomorrow. What do your pals do?

A. Even though they're all totally fried from lack of sleep, they haul over to your house for a Sunday cram session.
B. Tell you you're on your own, they're too tired to be of any help to you.
C. Loan you their notes and then head home to crash.

How Great Are *Your* Friends?

Add up your score by checking your answers to this point system.

1. A = 2 points B = 3 points C = 1 point
2. A = 3 points B = 1 point C = 2 points
3. A = 1 point B = 2 points C = 3 points
4. A = 3 points B = 1 point C = 2 points

Now see how your group measures up:

0–5 points: Call it quits on the clique. They're not real friends at all.

6–9 points: You're hangin' with some cool kids, but you may not always be able to rely on them. You can still remain friends, but be ready for some tough times along the way.

10–12 points: Lucky you! These friends are true blue. Hope you are, too!

NANCY KRULIK HAS WRITTEN more than 150 books for children and young adults, including three *New York Times* bestsellers. She is the author of the popular Katie Kazoo Switcheroo series and is also well known as a biographer of Hollywood's hottest young stars. Her knowledge of the details of celebrities' lives has made her a desired guest on several entertainment shows on the E! network as well as on *Extra* and *Access Hollywood.* Nancy lives in Manhattan with her husband, composer Daniel Burwasser, their two children, Ian and Amanda, and a crazy cocker spaniel named Pepper.